Aoife's Journal - A Celtic Dream

by Philomena Digings

ISBN: 9798542948461

© Copyright 2021
All rights reserved

Thank you to artist, STIG TOMAS, for the use of a copy of his painting 'Angel' for the front cover. (Encaustic wax overlaid with pen and ink drawing)
Prints of this work and others are available for sale on his website: **www.artiesart.com**

Meet the author

That brilliant feminist writer, Gloria Steinem, was, like me, an avid reader at an early age. As Gloria said, in her books about becoming a writer, "I soon developed myopia and a firm belief that people in books were not only more interesting, but more real than people outside of books."

Whenever, anyone wanted to know where I was, it was likely that I was tucked away in my bedroom reading whatever I could get my hands on. Having been initiated into the art of reading through the dreaded 'Janet and John" series, I soon progressed to more interesting material from a wide range of books, such as Lewis Carroll's Alice series, C.S. Lewis' 'The Lion, The Witch and the Wardrobe', Johanna Spyri's Heidi series, Noel Streatfeild's Ballet Shoes and the heartbreaking story of Anne Frank.

I investigated the 'classics' my dad had on our book shelves at home. These were mostly from his own youth. Writers such as John Buchan, Rudyard Kipling, JRR Tolkein, et al.
Later I met The Brontes, George Orwell, Virginia Woolf, Anthony Burgess and many more. I was introduced to Shakespeare, firstly through 'Lamb's Tales of Shakespeare' and later through a performance of 'Midsummer's Nights Dream'.

I also developed an interest in the role of women in mythological stories and legends. As my mother, 'mam', was Irish, I found a fascination for the strong female characters that existed in many folk tales, especially those from Ireland. They stand out as exceptional because, in more recent centuries, they have come to be regarded as different from the social and cultural 'norms' of their time. The stories were from an oral tradition, but recorded in writing centuries later. The earlier versions, passed down the generations, emphasised the importance of female deities. The later written accounts were recorded by Christian writers, notably monks and those connected with the Church. In these versions, the focus was rather on male deities and their greater importance.

All my books can be found on Amazon in paperback and Kindle formats.

See my website: **www.wordsflypast.com**

Find me on Facebook at wordsflypast

Also by the same author:

- White Swan, Black Swan (2021) Detective story – set in 1965. Detective Constable Anna KInsale's second case.

- Machinations, Malpractice and Murder (2020) Detective story – set in 1965. Detective Constable Anna KInsale's first case.

- A trilogy of semi-autobiographical novels:

  - Wild Waves and Dragon's Song (2018)
  - Planting Footsteps in the Sea (2019)
  - Oceana (2020)

- A bridge to Childhood (2019) - memories of a 1950s childhood.

- The Centre Cannot Hold (2017) – political thriller set in 1960s/70s.

- Conglomeration (2015) – a collection of my own poetry.

(1) Meet Aoife Ryan

Date: 2021.

> *"Goin' up to the spirit in the sky*
> *That's where I'm gonna go when I die*
> *When I die and they lay me to rest*
> *I'm gonna go to the place that's the best."*

(Norman Greenbaum, song, 1969)

Let me introduce myself. My name is Aoife Ryan. I'm 68 years old. In this book, you will find that I have chosen extracts to present from my journal. Some are from childhood. From my 12th birthday until I was 16 years old. I decided not to record these in chronological order, but rather as I felt they naturally fell into the story. I have also included what I call my 'musings'. I have dated all these as this year of writing, 2021. In fact, some were written at different times during my adulthood. I include them as reflections on happenings in my life, but also as explanations and background to put my own experiences into some kind of context !

I am an only child. That said, for all my life I have lived alongside other sisters. How ?

Well, I was a lone child in my family, just my Mam and my Da and me. This continued until I was 12 years old.

'What happened then ?' you may ask.

I had a visitation from another *Aoife* from the Otherworld on my 12th birthday. Later I met my second sister, *Banba*. I also met *Epona* an equine goddess and *Faoladh*, my lupine protector.

From then on, my life with my two supernatural sisters and the other characters I have been in contact with, both in and from, the Otherworld, have remained with me and run parallel to, often integral to, my Earthly life. I became, what is known by those lucky enough to have these relations, a True Believer.

The 'Spirit in the Sky' in Norman Greenbaum's song was influenced by his experience meeting Hopi Native Americans. For them, the 'Great Spirit' is the concept of a life force, a Supreme Being, or a god who created Our World here on Earth. When this work began, he created other gods to help him in the momentous task.

Here in Ireland, we have a multiplicity of Celtic gods and goddesses, who can act together or independently. They can change their physical form from humanoid, to animal or even elements of nature or weather, such as trees or thunderstorms. Certain gods and goddesses control natural elements.

We also have Druids with Celtic origins. My Da, now aged 93, is one of such a group. They too, believe in a Great Spirit. The Druids believe that the soul is immortal and passed on at death from one person into another. Druidism exists in a modern spiritual, religious movement that generally promotes harmony, connection, and reverence for the natural world. Another prominent belief among modern Druids is the veneration of ancestors, particularly those who belonged to ancient societies.

On my 12th birthday, my parents gave me the present of a diary which had a page for each day of the year. They knew I loved writing stories and encouraged me to write from personal experience, as well as from my imagination. I have kept up this writing in the form of a journal. Now I have 56 years worth of my own writing.

A friend suggested a while ago that this work should be read and possibly celebrated by others. I have selected extracts which I feel have a relevance to, or interest for, other people. I hope I can demonstrate how my own reception and understanding of all the issues which have developed over my lifetime make sense to me. They have opened my mind and led me to progression and enlightenment. As I grow older, I trust that a rebirth in some form will await me after my physical death.

I have tried to be selective in choosing the extracts after reflection As I don't intend to compete with 'War and Peace', or Proust's 'À la Recherche du Temps Perdu', (Remembrance of Things Past) in terms of numbers of words, I have chosen to break up my journal extracts and my accompanying reviewing comments, into several separate books.

This is the first and covers the period from my 12th Birthday and my introduction to the Otherworld, up until my 16th Birthday, which takes me to the age known in the Druid calendar as being on the cusp of womanhood. It was here where things began to change quite significantly. But firstly, here, I look back at what happened earlier on.

Looking back, I think that from a very early age, I knew there was something special, different, about my parents. There were other children who belonged to the True Believers' community. We don't call ourselves a 'sect' or 'denomination', as we live our lives in a looser, more open way than such terms might imply. Our aim is to be at one with the natural world and listen to what it has to tell us. This is something that the whole human race should be focussing on at the moment in view of global warming, climate change and the pollution caused to our planet by industrialisation.

Pollution takes many forms. It affects the air we breathe, the water we drink, the soil we use to grow our food and the skies which are now full of vapour trails and artificial light. Even the constantly increasing noises, like traffic, that we hear daily in towns and cities, contribute to health problems and a lower quality of life with major disruptions and effects on wildlife and ecosystems. Sadly, this has worsened in my lifetime. Humans in general have lost contact with nature. As a population, people need to learn to respect their environment and learn to heal and repair the damage caused;

One of the greatest problems that our Earthly world is facing today is that of environmental pollution. It's causing serious and irreparable damage to our beautiful, natural world. In addition, in human society, together with over-population, over 3 billion people suffer malnutrition. True Believers and their Otherworldly companions, believe that a polluted environment creates a polluted society. It's one we humans created and only we can renew.

The characters from the Otherworld have taken me beyond the realms of this world and given me a glimpse into another; an elsewhere which is mysterious and magical. It is infinite. No-one can explore the whole. You just follow what you are guided towards by an Otherworldly being, an Earthly teacher and your own intellect or instinct. I'm still not sure whether there's any great pre-destined plan beyond my understanding. Some might say that I have conjured up my journeys and my relationships outside of human company in my own imagination.

Certainly, place has had a powerful influence on me. Not just Earthly places like where you are born and where you spend your childhood and adulthood. These are indeed very important to me. The experiences of childhood have remained with me for life. The happiness of family, the enjoyment of the companionship of friends and adventures, notably through the interconnection with beings from beyond this realm. It has formed my adulthood. The older I get, the more memories I have and the more I possess which can be drawn upon to convey me along the path of existence wherever that takes me.

I have, together with my Mam, now 91, studied the history and progression of the females I am writing about in my journal, both Earthly, from past and present, as well as Otherworldly, often in the form of goddesses. Those I have chosen, or who have chosen me, stand out as exceptional. I could say because they are, in certain key ways, outside the social and cultural 'norms' of the Earthly times in which I live. They have strength and power. Certainly not the caged birds of this poem by Paul Laurence Dunbar *(1872-1906),* although that was likely the fate of many women across the centuries and, sadly, still is today in some cultures.

Sympathy

I know what the caged bird feels, alas!
When the sun is bright on the upland slopes;
When the wind stirs soft through the springing grass,
And the river flows like a stream of glass;
When the first bird sings and the first bud opens,
And the faint perfume from its chalice steals—
I know what the caged bird feels!
I know why the caged bird beats its wing
Till its blood is red on the cruel bars;
For he must fly back to his perch and cling
When he fain would be on the bough a-swing;
And a pain still throbs in the old, old scars
And they pulse again with a keener sting—
I know why he beats his wing!
I know why the caged bird sings, ah me,
When his wing is bruised and his bosom sore,—
When he beats his bars and he would be free;
It is not a carol of joy or glee,
But a prayer that he sends from his heart's deep core,
But a plea, that upward to Heaven he flings -
I know why the caged bird sings!

(Maya Angelou (1928-2014) was a black American poet, memoirist, and civil rights activist.)

It was Maya Angelou who introduced me to the metaphor of a bird struggling to escape its cage, described in Dunbar's poem. The poem brings vividly to life a symbol representing imprisonment. In Angelou's case, through race and oppression. The caged bird metaphor invokes the apparent contradiction of the bird singing in the midst of its struggle. How conscious is the bird of its lack of liberty ? It could be argued that if the bird knows no other environment, then it shouldn't be bothered. Conversely, is there something in the bird's spirit that tells it this isn't right ? If it senses something's wrong, does it give in to loss of freedom ? Or does it revolt against its captors ? Is the singing a complaint, a comfort, or a song of simple joy at being alive ?

For Maya Anglou, she gradually found that her imprisonment in a racist society contained a sequence of lessons about resisting oppression. The sequence of events in her life led her, as she describes it from "helpless rage and indignation to forms of subtle resistance, and finally to outright and active protest".

The same questions could be asked of 'The Stepford Wives', the 1972 satirical novel by Ira Levin which later, in 1975, was released as a film. I'd describe it as an American satirical horror story. The main character, Joanna Eberhart, is a photographer and young mother. She comes to suspect that the submissive housewives in her new idyllic Connecticut neighbourhood may be robots created by their husbands. It is an indictment of the white, middle-class, American womanhood of the post World War Two decades. During WW2, women got a taste of freedom in new wartime roles. Afterwards, it was time for men to put them back in their place ! In the book, a group of dominant misogynists, realising they can't control their wives, replace them with 'ideal woman' robots !

The main Earthly characters featured in my life story, are myself , (Aoife), my Mam (Macha) and my Da (Dagda)

The Otherworldly characters are:

- *Aoife* is my first Otherworld sister and namesake. She appears as a character in the Ulster Cycle of Irish mythology and stories are told of her in the sagas *Tochmarc Emire* (the wooing of Emer) and *Aided Óenfhir Aífe* (the death of *Aoife*'s only son). She is central to my life and the stories in my journal.

- My second sister is *Banba*, the sovereign lady of Ireland. *Banba* 'owns', or rather 'oversees', the natural world of Ireland in all its forms: plants, animals and humans. She is also known as the Mother of Ireland. She has also had the name of Ériu. She is still interpreted as a modern-day personification of Ireland, although since the name "Ériu" is the older Irish form of the word Ireland, her modern name is often modified to "Éire" or "Erin" to suit a modern form. She is the daughter of *Delbáeth* and *Ernmas* of the *Tuatha Dé Danann*. a supernatural race in Irish mythology. They are thought to represent the main deities of pre-Christian Gaelic Ireland. The *Tuatha Dé Danann* constitutes a supernatural group whose attributes appear in a number of forms throughout the ancient Celtic world and beyond. For a time, *Banba* was married to *Mac Cuill*, a grandson of the *Dagda*.

- *Epona* is another Celtic goddess I have met and travelled with. Her name contains an allusion to the horse: in Celtic, "epos" means 'horse" and the suffix "ona" simply means 'on'. *Epona* is the patron goddess of mares and foals. The oldest information about *Epona*, goddess of horses, is found in Juvenal's writing. Decimus Junius Juvenalis, known in English as Juvenal, was a Roman poet active in the late 1st and early 2nd centuries AD. He is the author of a collection of satirical poems known as 'The Satires'. There is reference to *Epona* in this work. I write about several personal interactions with her in my journal.

- For my Mam, her goddess and Otherworldly sister is her namesake, *Macha*. Several figures called *Macha* appear in Irish mythology and folklore, all believed to derive from the same goddess. She is said to be one of three sisters known as 'the three *Morrígna*'. Like other sovereignty goddesses, *Macha* is associated with the land, fertility, kingship, war and, particularly horses.

- My Da's Otherworldly brother is the god *Dagda* who was the son of *Danu*, the 'mother goddess' and *Elatha*, the King of the *Fomorians*. These are a supernatural race in Irish mythology. They are often portrayed as hostile and monstrous beings who come from under the sea or the Earth. They have also been portrayed as giants and sea raiders. *Dagda* is the eldest and wisest of the *Tuath Dé Danann*, another supernatural race in Irish mythology. This race are thought to represent the main deities established in pre-Christian Gaelic Ireland. *Dagda* is considered to be not only a father figure, but also the Druid of the tribe. *Dagda* eventually became the King of the *Tuatha Dé Danann*. *Dagda* is not only a god of great power and prestige, but is also thought of in a comical way. I'm sure my Da inherited his sense of humour, as he's a great joker. Unfortunately, *Dagda*, in his original form, died of poisoning by the wife of an enemy named *Balor*, during the battle of *Magh Tuiredh*. *Dagda* was reborn and remains a very similar character. My Da always jokes that he should have a food taster whenever Mam serves up a meal, just in case !

(2) The Celtic Dream begins . . .

Date: <u>Infinitude</u>

> The host is riding from Knocknarea
> And over the grave of Clooth-na-Bare;
> Caoilte tossing his burning hair,
> And Niamh calling Away, come away:
> Empty your heart of its mortal dream.
> The winds awaken, the leaves whirl round,
> Our cheeks are pale, our hair is unbound,
> Our breasts are heaving, our eyes are agleam,
> Our arms are waving, our lips are apart;
> And if any gaze on our rushing band,
> We come between him and the deed of his hand,
> We come between him and the hope of his heart.
> The host is rushing 'twixt night and day,
> And where is there hope or deed as fair?
> Caoilte tossing his burning hair,
> And Niamh calling Away, come away.

(The Hosting of the Sidhe" by W. B. Yeats)

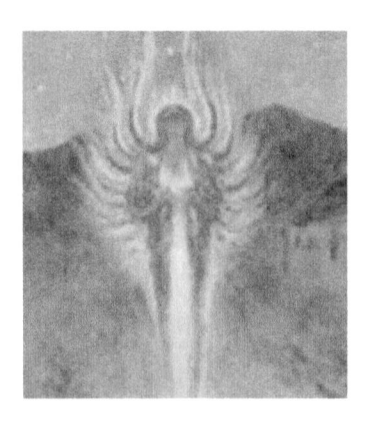

The time has come for the human child, Aoife, *to meet her Otherworldly partner. We, the Sidhe, as you call us, are the fairy folk and mythological beings and creatures who exist both in your world and our own dimensions, which are many. You also use your a Gaelic word to mean 'The Wind' to describe us. You are right. We are a natural, everyday force, yet we are magical figures. It is us who instil all natural forces with a mystical air.*

We will beckon the human child, not just to the land of the eternal and immortal, but will also invites her to experience an opportunity to escape sometimes from the realm of the ordinary into the extraordinary. The land of we Otherwordly beings is "Calling Away, Come Away" to the human child Aoife.

Aoife, the bright and radiant one, will invite her to open her heart to not just its mortal dream, but a dream into infinity. Freedom from the mundane. Exciting and irresistible for a child on the brink of adulthood. It is written that she will follow this invitation to step outside of the reality of the moment. The wind will awaken her and the leaves will whirl and the waters will swirl around her.

Aoife, *the human child, will know and experience the wildness and freedom associated with our Irish mythology. She will open like a flower already in bud. We, The Sidhe, will evoke in her the excitement of being at one with the supernatural and the mystical of the Otherworld. Accept, do not question, the magic of the Sidhe.*

Where are you from ? you ask. We, The Sidhe, inhabit an unconfined, everlasting place that combines the Earthly with the Unearthly. Some may doubt the existence of the place or we beings, but they are the ones who shall miss out. This extra dimension is granted to those who are ready to believe. We know that young Aoife *will grasp her opportunity enthusiastically and welcome her sister from the Otherworld with open arms. Those who are open to seeing will embrace us in their lives and minds. We offer an infinite space for possibilities and suggestions. Nothing is clear, but that's exactly the key. The world of fairy magic may be too much to resist, but we can promise her that it will be worth it and reward her with more than she could have imagined. Aoife is Calling Away, Come Away…….*

───────────────────────────────

(3) Aoife Ryan Muses

At the age of 9, poet William Blake saw what he interpreted as an angel. He wrote a poem about the experience later in life in 1794.

> "I Dreamt a Dream! what can it mean?
> And that I was a maiden Queen:
> Guarded by an Angel mild:
> Witless woe, was ne'er beguil'd!
>
> And I wept both night and day
> And he wip'd my tears away
> And I wept both day and night
> And hid from him my hearts delight
>
> So he took his wings and fled:
> Then the morn blush'd rosy red:
> I dried my tears & armed my fears,
> With ten thousand shields and spears.
>
> Soon my Angel came again;
> I was arm'd, he came in vain:
> For the time of youth was fled,
> And grey hairs were on my head."

(William Blake 1757-1827) English poet, painter, and printmaker.)

Date: 2021.

I have found it interesting in recent years how many computer games have drawn on mythology, both the settings and the characters.

Back in the 1990s when I was beginning my experience with computers and the games available, I discovered Lara Croft from a game called 'Tomb Raider' which became available in 1996. She immediately struck me as bearing a strong resemblance to the warrior goddesses.

Lara Croft. (from company: Core Design)

She is presented as a highly intelligent and athletic English archaeologist who ventures into ancient tombs and hazardous ruins around the world. Lara was said to have been inspired by strong female icons with a view to countering stereotypical female characters. Of course, she has since been followed by a range and variety of characters with similar characteristics. Great for girls !

More recently, 'Dragon Age' is centred around a series of fantasy role-playing video games. The action in these games takes place on the fictional continent of Thedas and follows the experiences of its various inhabitants. Race, class and heritage combine to determine social class and political dynamics in the domain of Thedas. For those who enjoy these technological games, it is an opportunity for them to experience life in a different dimension. By opening their minds to alternative worlds, perhaps it's another, modern, way of reaching out into the Otherworld and making contact with those who exist in the Ether.

The women I mention, both Earthly and Otherworldly, including myself, do not always follow the rules of their society. For example, my Mam, *Macha*, was a nurse and continued to work after having children. What we would call today, a 'working mum'. In the 1950s and 60s, this would not have been thought usual in Ireland or the UK. All my young life, she encouraged me to be strong, open-minded and independent. She has helped me to manage the relationships across the boundaries between the mystical and everyday reality.

This parental attitude has been replicated by my Da, His fraternal Otherworldly being is the god, *Dagda*, after whom Da is named. As I've indicated, *The Dagda* is an important god in Irish mythology. He is portrayed as a father-figure, King, and Druid. Da is certainly a good father. He is also a Druid. Like his namesake, he is associated with fertility, agriculture, manliness and strength, as well as magic, Druidry and wisdom. Da comes from a farming background himself. His elder brother, my uncle, took over the farm when Granddad died. Da chose an academic course and is a history fellow at Dublin University. Not surprisingly, his specialism is Irish Celtic mythology and legend.

Over the 56 years in which I have continued to write my journal, I have found myself focussing on the women's story as a central theme. Certain questions have become essential in order to place us women, whether Earthly or Otherworldly, in the context of the age and place in which we live / have lived:

- What was, or isn't, permitted in our societies ?
- What were / are the rules which had to / have to be followed ?.

- How did /do different ideologies and laws impact on everyday life ?
- How were /are our identities shaped by our relationship with our parents and those around us ?
- How did / do we interact with our surreal goddesses ?
- What were/are the major influences which shaped the women they became / have become /will become ?

Over the years, I have attempted to answer these questions as best I can. At least to some extent ! I have come to realise that Unworldly beings don't want to spell out our future. It is each individual's task to open their mind to all possibilities. Spend each day as if it was your last – make the most of it. Never stop learning ever, for eternity.

The wonderful Mahatma Gandhi said, "Happiness is when what you think, what you say, and what you do are in harmony."

It's what *Aoife* has reiterated to me. When the Multiverse is in harmony, all is well. *Aoife* calls it polyphony. On Earth, it's a word we associate with music: the style of simultaneously combining a number of parts, each forming an individual melody and harmonising with each other.

Da is a Druid. I've discovered over my lifetime that there's a rich storehouse of inspiration in the teachings of Druidry. In the 21st century these are now more relevant than ever. It's because they address the most urgent and important issue of our time. That is how to galvanise all of our Human spiritual potential and the strength of those Beings from the Otherworld, who are more knowing than us, to protect and restore the Earth, which we have abused, to its true natural state. Only then can we move forward in a different way and be at one with the spirits of the natural world.

One thing about keeping a journal has sometimes been the problem, if I can call it that, of explaining and describing the things I have seen and experienced in words, in language. So much has been more to do with feelings, sensations. These are often so intense, so magical , that words seem inadequate. That said, maybe I'm a glutton for punishment, but I do love writing, especially creative writing ! I have tried over the years to relax and let the phenomena, once experienced, to continue a life of its own, using me as a kind of secretary, taking up the pen and recording the happenings both in a general and personal sense.

In fact, over my life, it has been helpful for me to put the Otherworldly characters into a more general context, as well as their relationship to me. Although perceptions of what might be called goddesses, angels, supernatural brings, aliens and so on, have changed over centuries, many of the stories related to them still exist in written form and in oral form through stories, songs and poems. It is these I have drawn on to make sense of the context in which I live and in which I write my journal.

Despite the changes made when recording these ancient stories from their oral genre and the fact that many oral versions of stories and early manuscripts have been lost in the mists of time, we are lucky in Ireland because four key sets, or 'Cycles' of stories remain. They are 'The Mythological', 'The Ulster', 'The Fenian' and 'The Historical'. Outside of these, other folk tales continue as oral stories, poems and songs repeated to generations of Irish. Many tales, both within or outside the Cycles, involve the same or similar characters and story lines.

Most 'goddesses' are linked to the natural world, the land and the sea. Often these are thought to originate from ancient ancestors of the indigenous peoples of an area. They may have a maternal role – caring, protecting and teaching. They are also portrayed as warriors. I have tried to explore this dual nature which has been seen as both good and bad, depending on who is writing or presenting the story and at what time in history.

(4) Aoife - a being of the Otherworld

Date: Infinitude.

I am Aoife. 'The Bright One'. I shine beauty and radiance. I am the flashes of light, which appear so brilliant in the sky, as I begin a thunderstorm and cocoon the Earth in black. As the thunder roars, it pours a molten silver shower which quenches the Earth. Upon the top of every thunderstorm is the light of the sun or stars. Let your dreams rise there in such times. Even in the dark you may see me. Concentrate your mind. Free it from distraction. I am a shining beacon.
Who am I ? I am a goddess, a woman of the Otherworld. I am Aoife, the daughter of Airdgeimm of Lethra. I have a number of sisters in spirit. Always in multiples of 3, a sacred number.

I was the twin sister of Scathach. We are both warrior women. Scathach is an expert trainer of warriors. Scathach is the ruler of an Otherworld kingdom called Tir na Scath. You would call it 'The Land of Shadows'. She is also known as 'The Shadow'. She lives in an enchanted fortress named Dun Scathach.

I am also the second of the wives of King Lir of Tullynally Caisteal. But that is a story in itself for another time.

How old am I ? By the time of Earth, I am more than centuries old. I go back in eons of time. Further than you could imagine. I die, yet I am reborn. I am both a time and a space traveller. I can appear on Earth, but I also exist in different, or parallel, dimensions. The strange thing about time travel is its limits. Like others of my kind, I can go forwards as far as I want, through the generations yet to come. I can go back. I may return. Nevertheless, we of the Otherworld do not change a Human's past. One Human's past may be another's future. We are continually reborn in other times and places. We move forward from wherever we are in the universe. I do not know how many we are. An infinite number.

On Earth, in my latest incarnation, I have chosen another sister. Aoife, a human child. I am part of her and she is part of me. Yet she can follow her own path. I can be one or two or three in one. I am only complete when I am three, or six, or nine……

Whilst this sister is young, I shall be her guide and show her the way. Already, I have whispered in the ear of the great Oisín, one of the Believers. In the Otherworld, Oisín is the greatest poet of Ireland. His stories survive and are told and retold. He has smiled upon this transition. Soon, I shall introduce myself to her upon her 12th birthday, for that is the right time. (4 seasons x 3)

I hope that I can guide young Aoife towards an epiphany. When she has full understanding of her inter-relationships with those of us from the Otherworld, there will be a time where she experiences a life-changing moment of self-understanding; an illumination of all the possibilities that exist in the macrocosm.

We gods and goddesses have had close relationships with the Celtic people for ever. Many of them are True Believers. They are a society of independent thinking minds. Importantly, they also have a natural mysticism. The Celts have also been known for their tendency for being progressive. This can be seen in their early laws, where females have equality with males. Yet, they do not turn their backs on traditions dating back to pre-Christianity.

There is a strong and important inter-relatedness between we goddesses of the Otherworld and Human woman. The source of all life, both here and there, is that from women. The very origins of life are female. We know that humans turn to us in times of need. We goddesses are honoured in all our guises. It should not be considered strange to worship a female deity. That being the case, we should, in turn, treat our female subjects with respect and honour. Motherhood, across the multiverse is a key element in the social fabric of any society. Keeping traditions and following allegiance to their goddesses, will help members of Earthly societies to open their minds to the wonders which lie ahead. I, Aoife, will guide and support my young, human sister in her journey through her Earthly life and prepare her for the life to come.

(5) Aoife Ryan - an Earthly Child

Date: 1965.

My name's *Aoife* Ryan. It's my birthday today, the 1st November 1965. I'm 12 years old. My name is Irish. In English, you'd pronounce it 'EE-FA'. My Da teases me and says I got the name because I appeared out of the 'ether'! My friend, Caoimhe (pronounced 'kee-va') says it's because when my Mam was expecting me, they didn't know if I'd be a girl or a boy, so they called me Aoife, short for 'either'. Caoimhe's name comes from the Gaelic word 'caomh', a name meaning gentle, beautiful or precious, as she keeps telling me. I still prefer my name. It's derived from the Gaelic word, 'aoibh', which means 'beauty' or 'radiance'.

We have a copy of a painting of Aoife, by the artist John Duncan, in our living room. I am blue-eyed and have golden hair, like my namesake. It's why my Mam, Macha, bought it when she saw it for sale. She told me it called to her.

Aoife as imagined by John Duncan, a Scottish artist – 1866 – 1945)

The Goddess Macha, who my Mam is named after.

Like her namesake, *Macha*, my Mam, loves horses and is a keen rider. My Grandpa Ryan was a blacksmith. Mam remembers there were always horses around her home, including her own pony, which all the children in the family shared. It was named *Macha*, after the horse goddess who could run like the wind.

Did you know that in Celtic Astrology, the Wolf is
the Celtic animal sign for people born between October 28th
and November 4th ? I was born on 1st November, so the wolf
is my Celtic Animal Zodiac Sign. My characteristics are that I
am, or will be, a natural teacher and give guidance to others.
Da's a teacher, so I might follow in his footsteps. I am fiercely
loyal to both friends and family. Something exciting, which ties
in with reading about Irish mythology is that I will experience
change during my life and rebirth when I die.

I love reading, so does Da. I am also inheriting his love of
Celtic history, He read me a story about the origin of my
name. He explained that *Aoife* is a character from the 'Ulster
Cycle' of Irish mythology. She is a goddess and a warrior
queen and married to King *Lir*. *Lir* means 'sea' in the Old Irish
language. *King Lir* is a sea god. In mythology, he also
represents the sea itself. He is a god who can change into
water. Da says there are a lot of beings, that we think of as
gods and goddesses, like this in ancient myths and legends
from all over the world. They are called 'shape-shifters'.

My namesake, *Aoife* appears in two sagas. The first one is called '*Tochmarc Emire*' and the other one is '*Aided Óenfhir Aife*'. In the first story, part of her life is spent to the east of Ireland in a land called *Alpi or Alba.* This is what we now call Scotland.

I love reading in bed before I go to sleep. I drift off imagining the Otherworld and all the beings and creatures who live there. Tonight, after a lovely birthday party and a delicious cake, I am in bed, tired but contented. I make the first notes in my new journal, a birthday present from Mam and Da.

I am just dozing off when I see through the curtains a flash of light. It's followed by a roar of thunder. I love thunderstorms. I get up to watch. Pushing back the curtains, a flash of lightning zigzags across the sky. From the window, I watch the ancient oak tree at the end of the garden silhouetted against the sky. I know it will stand firm in every thunderstorm. On the top of the thunderstorm is the sparkling light of the stars. I let my dreams and imaginings rise there, high above the storm. The lightning is enchanting. The streaks of bold light electrify my heart.

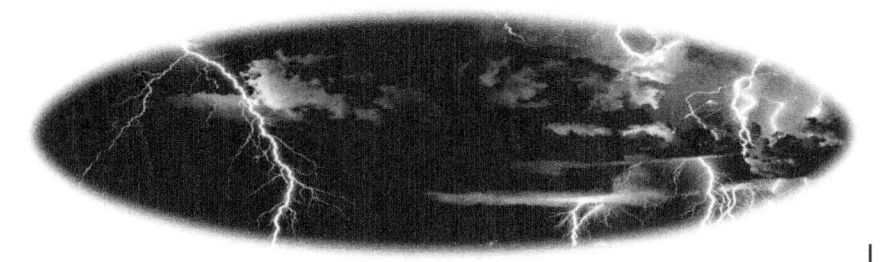

It's as if the lightning is recharging my soul while the rain is cleansing me and the whole Earth. The thunder resonates deep in my bones.

When the storm has passed, I return to my bed. Sleep will not come. I close my eyes and will myself to go to sleep. As I almost succeed, I hear a voice calling me.

"*Aoife. Aoife*".

Instantly, my eyes open. Standing, or rather hovering, in my room, in front of the window, where the raindrops are still pelting against the glass, is a misty figure, like a will-o'-the-wisp. As I watch, she appears more clearly. She looks like me, but very pale, as if she was cold, even icy. Pale skin. Hair golden. Soaked in shining crystals. Her body seems like floating chiffon. Not solid. A person with the shape and texture of a cloud. Is she a ghost ? An angel ?

"A voice emerges from the wispy shape. "Don't be afraid, *Aoife*".

"Who are you ?" I ask, fascinated, but frightened.

" I am *Aoife*. You are me and I am you. I am. We are. I have watched you since you were born. You were destined to be *Aoife*."

I don't understand. I feel excited, but nervous. "What are you doing here ?"

"I know you have never heard nor seen me in your life. Now, you are old enough. Twelve is the age for you to begin to understand. The age is chosen because there are 4 seasons in the year, Spring, Summer, Autumn and Winter. As a goddess, I have the ability to become three beings, or six or nine. I lost a sister, but that is another story. Now, I am only two. I seek another sister who matches me in spirit.

At present, as well as myself, there is a goddess named *Banba*. She lives invisibly in your world in what is called 'The Woodland'. She is a creature of nature; a protector of the natural world. She is Mother Erin."

I am speechless. I don't know what to say.

" I can appear in any world," continues the figure. " Now you too are *Aoife*, living on Earth. We three; me, yourself and *Banba* are as triplets. Three is a lucky number. Multiply the seasons by three and you have your age. Do you see ?"

I nod warily. "I think so."

"I have watched you, cared for you, healed you. Your soul is ready. It is a treasure wanted in the Otherworld. I will help you make your way into the light."

"Am I going to die ?" I ask, feeling my lips tremble and tears forming in my eyes.

The figure laughs. A gentle sound. "No. You will live a long and happy life as *Aoife,* a human on Earth. I live in the Otherworld, while you are here in your world. I will visit you from time to time. When it is right, you will visit me. I shall send a messenger."

I say nothing, trying to take it all in.

"Something you must look for when you are out walking is a four-leafed clover. In the place known as The Woodland, they may be gathered at night-time whenever there is a full moon. *Banba*, who is also a sorceress, mixes them with the plant, vervain and other magical ingredients. When I was your age, *Banba*, who is a magical one you might think of as a fairy, whispered in my ear that if you sup the mixture containing a four-leaf clover, the first leaf represents hope, the second stands for faith, the third is for love and the fourth leaf brings luck to the finder. She will confirm this when you meet. Fear not if she offers you a bowl of the liquid."

There are so many questions I want to ask. Curiosity has overcome fear. I open my mouth to speak, but I see *Aoife* put her finger to her lips.

"Enough for now, child. I will visit you again and you will visit me."

Her body fades and becomes a haze dancing in the air. Then, as if the window was open, she vanishes to the outside and is gone.

I sit bolt upright on the bed. Was this some kind of magical dream ? …………..

The next day, while I am mulling over this visitation, I am planning how I will record it in my journal, I think I should write about myself first.

<u>My Journal</u>

Date: 2nd November 1965

My name is Aoife Ryan. I live in the countryside in County Cork in Ireland. There is a wood not far from my home and I wonder if I will find my other new sister, *Banba*, the Goddess of Nature, living here, close to home.

I live near Blarney. It's a village outside the city of Cork. It's famous for Blarney Castle, built in the 15th century. The castle is home to the legendary Blarney Stone. ('*Cloch na Blarnan*') It's said to give the "gift of the gab" to those who kiss it. That means the gift of being both eloquent and persuasive ! It's a tradition that's been around for centuries. The stone is set in a wall of the castle. The castle is known for its mystery and magic.

Once upon a time, visitors had to be held by the ankles and lowered head first over the battlements. My Mam and Da did just this ! Today, the guardians of the castle are rather more cautious about the safety of visitors. The Stone itself is still set in the wall below the battlements. To kiss it, you have to lean backwards, whilst holding onto an iron railing from the parapet walk. I have to wait until I'm a bit taller before I am allowed to try it. I will do it though !!

We learnt in school that Blarney castle was originally built way back, before the year 1200. It was a wooden structure then. Around 1210, this wooden building was replaced by a stone fortification which was, unfortunately, destroyed in 1446. The castle was rebuilt the same year by Cormac Láidir MacCarthy (1411-1494) He was an Irish chieftain and Lord of Muscry. He is best known for constructing three castles: Kilcrea Castle, Carrignamuck Tower House, and Blarney Castle. He also discovered and enshrined the Blarney Stone.

There are many myths and legends surrounding the Blarney Stone itself. It dates back into the mists of time. One, that Da told me, involved the goddess *Clíodhna,* who endowed the Stone with its power and passed it on to Cormac Laidir MacCarthy. The story goes that he was troubled with a lawsuit. He feared the ruling would go against him and he might lose his position as Lord of Muscry. He prayed to the goddess *Clíodhna*.

She came to him one night and told him to kiss the first stone that he found on the way to the Court. In the morning, he did as he was bidden. He kissed the first stone he found. To his amazement, he immediately was given the "gift of the gab". Sure enough, he won his case in Court. Afterwards he brought the stone back and ordered it to be built into the parapet of the Castle. The stone is also known as 'the Stone of Eloquence'.

Blarney Castle (the stone is at the top under the crenellations)

Our castle holds the record for being one of the most 'haunted' places in Ireland. Once it had been built in stone, it became an important stronghold in medieval Irish history. After Cormac Laidir MacCarthy, Lord of Muscry, died, the castle was sieged, sold and changed hands many times. In the 1700s, Sir James St. John Jefferyes, the governor of Cork CIty, bought it. The Jefferyes family built a baronial mansion on the property, known as the Blarney House.

Today, only some of the Castle survives intact, with a few accessible rooms and, of course, the battlements. At the top of the castle lies the Stone of Eloquence, better known as the Blarney Stone. Tourists visiting Blarney Castle are usually keen to hang upside-down over a sheer drop to kiss the stone, which as I have said to give the gift of eloquent speech, or as some would put it, the "the gift of gab." There are many legends as to the origin of the stone, but some say that it was the Lia Fáil, which was a magical stone upon which Irish kings were crowned. Others believed that the goddess of Clíodhna provided it to help a warrior (who lacked good communication skills) in convincing Queen Elizabeth I from seizing the Castle. With this spell, he succeeded.

If you go below the tower house of Blarney Castle, you will find a labyrinth of underground passages and chambers. These are believed to have been the Castle's prison.

The Blarney Stone is not the only attraction. People say it is haunted by many of those who took part in its long history. Not everyone knows about, or understands, the spiritual and Otherworldly element of the Castle. Visitors are encouraged to listen closely, to hear the disembodied voices and footsteps that 'haunt' this estate. Mam, Dad and me know better. We are True Believers.

Visitors are told to be sure to go to the Witch's Kitchen. The owners of the castle truly believe that this was home to the very first Irish cave dwellers across the mists of time. If you arrive as dawn is breaking, you will see the dying embers of a fire. This fire has not been lit by any mortal during the night. This is lit every night by the Blarney Castle witch, as she fights to stop shivering on her nocturnal escape from the Witch Stone.

The castle is also known for being cursed. The Blarney Castle curse states that if a stone, rock, or even a pebbles, is removed from the area, it will bring misfortune and misery to whoever possesses it. Many ballads, poems and stories have spoken of the consequences of taking such natural treasures home. Strangely, over time, parcels were received by the Castle, returning stones that had been taken. Letters within the parcels speak of unexplained grief and tough times which have occurred since taking the stone/s.

There is an extensive parkland surrounding the castle. This is open to anyone and there's a whole network of trails to follow. Da says the grounds are whimsical and mysterious. Signs point visitors to natural rock formation spots to explore, including the Druid's Circle, Witch's Cave, and the Wishing Steps. The gardens are laid out formally in different styles, opening onto the big, turreted building, known as Blarney House.

The nuns at my school believe the Blarney Stone goes all the way back to the Prophet Jeremiah. It is said that the Blarney Stone was originally the stone of Jacob from the Book of Genesis and was brought to Ireland by the Prophet Jeremiah. The stone was first used in Ireland as an 'oracular throne'. The seat was a gift from an angel known as a 'Throne'.
An angel is a celestial being that acts as an intermediary between Heaven and Earth. Angelic beings are usually benevolent in nature and considered to manifest the qualities of goodness, purity, and selflessness. Seraphim are the highest order in the Hierarchy of Angels. Cherubim are the second highest order. Thrones are the third ranking order of angels. Dominiums are the fourth ranking order of angels. So the throne is like a chair of state for a king or high-ranking person, someone with royal power and dignity, who is approved by God.

It also was known as the *'Lia Fail'* (fatal stone). It was said to serve as the deathbed pillow for St Columba before being removed to the mainland of Scotland.

Some say, a previous Lord of Muscry, an ancestor of Conan McCarthy, sent 5,000 men to aid Robert the Bruce and Scotland in their fight against the English at the Battle of Bannockburn in 1314. They believe the Blarney Stone to be a piece of the Stone of the Scone, (stone of destiny), which is the seating place of the first King of Scots (Kenneth I MacAlpin, in old gaelic, *'Cináed mac Ailpín)* during his coronation in 847. The stone is said to be gifted to Ireland as a thank you for supporting Scotland at the battle.

Whatever the truth, its origins are mysterious.

The McCarthy's were not only powerful leaders and warriors, they were also patrons of Irish culture, music and art. They established a Bardic School at Blarney, which attracted scholars from throughout Ireland. By the 1600's, Blarney had become well known as a Court of Poetry where poets gathered to read their compositions, many of which have survived in the original old Irish form. My Da has read many of these and related the stories to me, explaining what they tell us about those mysterious times.

---

(6) The Nature and Status of Goddesses and Women

My Journal - Date: 2021.

During my Earthly life cycle, *Aoife* and *Banba* have taught me a huge amount. Together with what I have learned from reading and tales told to me by my darling Da, I know much. As I make clear throughout this journal, the ancient Celts in Ireland and elsewhere, focused on female deities. often concentrating on the dominant role of the Celtic female. She was honoured and respected. The myths and legends of their culture have been carried on up until today and are respected by True Believers and Druids alike.

The evolution of these stories has also changed the original sense of them. Originally passed down generations through their oral telling, they were later transcribed into written form. Here, they began to demonstrate a distinct shift in attitude and presentation. The warrior ethos becomes more closely linked with Christianity and patriarchy.

Sacred female goddesses, or mythical beings, revered for millennia, become, in medieval times, presented as unnaturally violent. Their matriarchal, life-giving qualities are gradually changed into being the bringers of death and destruction.

By the medieval period, the independent, strong women of the old Celtic society, who had enjoyed much freedom and equal status with men, became victims and often suffered at the hands of male violence for their 'ungodly' ways.

The goddess in ancient, pre-Christian Celtic society was a dual-natured, even two-faced, female figure. Even though she might be beautiful and good, she could change herself into an ugly and evil crone or hag. This ability meant she could metamorphose from one to the other, thus tricking people into believing she was benign, then turning the tables. It's worth remembering that, at this time, however, being a female warrior, was an admirable thing. Think of bravery and chivalry.

When I first encountered my Otherworldly sister, *Aoife,* at the age of 12, this concept of a dual nature was difficult to grasp. Of course, I understood the difference between good and bad, but at this young age, I suppose I saw things very much in black and white. It was why, after reading about this supernatural *Aoife* when I was a child, I was worried about how her actions seemed to fluctuate between jealous, or warlike and being empathetic, even affectionate.

The goddesses were especially depicted in trios. For example, I have mentioned *Banba* , the goddess who is my second sister. She oversees the land known as Ireland; looks after the natural world. She is sovereign of all the land in Ireland. She is believed to have acquired the name '*Eire*', the Irish name for Ireland, from a form of *Eriu,* another of her sisters.

Some Celtic goddesses seem to share a few of the characteristics of earlier goddesses from Greek and Roman culture. Interestingly, I discovered there are no Celtic goddesses of love. Celtic goddesses are more often associated with fertility and the natural cycle of life. They also represent creativity in the creation, life and death of all life on Earth and in the Otherworld.

---

(7) Faoladh The Wolfboy

Date: Spring 1966

A being from The Otherworld watches the sleeping child, Aoife. As moonlight shines through the window and onto the girl, the white creamy tone of her skin reminds him of pearls. He can't help but wonder if he reaches out, will he only touch air. As if she were nothing but a ghost.

Faoladh the Wolf – young Aoife's guardian

"*Aoife. Aoife,*" a voice whispers.

I am in bed. At first, I think Mam is calling me, but it's not her voice. This is a voice that sounds more like Da's, but it's a bit growlier. I hear it again.

"*Aoife. Aoife, wake up.*"

I open my eyes. I look round. I look at the mantelpiece opposite my bed. There are my 3 teddy bears, *Eion, Callum* and *Aiden*, sitting on there together with my dolls, *Aisling* and *Rhiannon*. Sitting, or I should say floating, just above them, is a strange looking toy. It's like a wolf. He's surrounded by mist, floating around him. He moves in and out of my sight. I should be scared, but I know somehow he's friendly and won't hurt me.

"Hello Aiofe. I'm *Faoladh*. Don't be afraid, I'm your friend."

"Where did you come from ?"

"I live in the sky in the constellation of Lupus . I am a wolf. I am a protector of children, people who are wounded and those who are lost."

I don't know what to say.

He continues. "Do you know of my home ?"

I shake my head, unable to think what to say or do.

He explains. "Lupus contains two stars with known planets. The brightest star in the constellation is Alpha Lupi, There are no meteor showers associated with my constellation. Lupus does not contain any formally named stars by your Earthly astronomers."

I struggle to understand what he is saying. It sounds very scientific to me. I nod politely.

He continues, pointing to the sky. The Lupus constellation lies in the southern hemisphere between Centaurus and Scorpius. Its name means "the wolf" in the language you call Latin.

I understand this because our Catholic Masses are spoken in Latin and I study Latin at school now.

"Lupus has been known on your planet for thousands of Earth years. Your Greek astronomer, Ptolemy, found us in the 2nd century of your time. We are an old constellation and home to several interesting stars and deep sky objects. Alpha Lupi, my own star, is the brightest star in the Lupus constellation. It is approximately 460 light years distant from Earth. "

"Wow, that's a huge distance," I exclaim. 'I have heard of light years."

Faoladh sighs happily. He is clearly proud of his home. "Mine is a blue-white giant star. It is ten times more massive than your Sun and about 25,000 times more luminous. Although the luminosity can vary due to pulsations in the atmosphere."

He notices that I look puzzled. "Don't worry, Aoife, I'm just showing off !"

There's a pause as we observe one another. As I watch, he changes. I'm amazed. His head and face remain the same, but the rest of the front of his body seems to have its lost its fur, a deep grey with specks of black. Now it has turned to skin. He has one leg furry and one leg made of skin.

I am frightened now.

He can sense that. "It's all right. I am a shape-shifter. Do you know what that means ?"

I do because I remember it from the mythical stories Da and I have read together. I nod.

He continues to change shape. Now he is a boy. Clothes have appeared on his body. Silver and gold sparkling through the swirling mist. He's about my age, but looks like a prince from a fairy tale. He beckons me over. I get out of bed, suddenly self-conscious because I'm only wearing my nightie.

Faoladh reaches out a hand and takes mine. He gently pulls me towards him. "Come," he says.

I float into the air and hover with him above the mantelpiece. The mist thickens and cocoons us. I feel myself changing. My golden hair has grown longer. I am wearing the clothes of a princess. A beautiful, cream-coloured, silken gown embroidered with silver and gold designs. It sparkles in the mist.

"Close your eyes," he instructs.

I obey. I feel myself lifting into the air. I panic. "Will I see Mam and Da again ? Where are we going ?"

"Shhh," he whispers.

Faoladh and Aoife

We rise. Above the house and on and up into the sky. We enter the clouds. Then higher still. It's night time. I can see stars. Across the deep darkness, there are thousands, maybe millions, of stars. Different sizes and shapes, swirling and flickering in the distance. The sky is so big. It seems to go on forever. It's like an enchanted world. If I focus on just one star, it plays hide and seek, disappearing behind an invisible cloud and then reappearing. The stars are like naughty children hiding away in the shadows and then, jumping out at you. I expect they will be there, playing for ever.

We descend. We reach a cloud and *Faoladh* guides me down. We sink slowly through the cloud and towards the ground. We land easily. I find myself standing on firm ground. It's daylight. Early morning with the sun rising over the horizon in shades of pink and orange and red.

Faoladh smiles at me.

I study him. *Faoladh*'s still a boy. "How old are you ?" I ask curiously.

"What do you think ?" he replies.

"My age ?"

He laughs. "When you look at me now, you see a boy. If you saw me in other forms, it would be hard to put an age on me. You can't guess my age because I change. I have changed over decades, even centuries. I don't know my age. I move across your world, but also the Otherworld. There are many worlds beyond your earth. I have travelled to places where time, as you know it, doesn't exist. There are ways of travelling through the universe according to different rules. For example, I can use wormholes to travel billions of miles."

"But wormholes are tiny ?"

He laughs. "A wormhole is a speculative structure linking disparate points in space time."

"I don't understand."

Faoladh reaches into the Ether and when his hand returns, it is holding a sheet of paper and a pencil. He smiles again.

" A way to imagine wormholes is to take a sheet of paper and draw two distant dots on the paper. Here, take the pencil."

He holds up the paper while I mark two dots. I put one at the top of the paper and one at the bottom so they are as far apart as possible. Is he going to do a magic trick ? I ask myself.

He nods. "That's it. Now, imagine, the sheet of paper represents part of the earth's surface, and the two dots you have drawn are two cities a long way apart. You could connect these two dots by folding that paper so the points are touching. The distance is far less now because you have created a tunnel with the folded paper which brings the cities closer together.

"But that's impossible !"

It is for you, but a tunnel like this, called a 'wormhole', can connect extremely long distances such as a billion light years or more. It would even work with short distances, just a few feet. On the other hand, we use it to visit different universes, or even different points in time. I could go away now and visit you when you are grown-up, even very old."

I find this hard to believe. We have learned about light travelling in science lessons at school. 186,000 miles a second, our teacher had told us. It was impossible to even imagine, yet here was this boy telling me that he and his kind could travel at such speeds ! That said, I have to remind myself that this boy can turn himself into an animal. I'd seen him change.

"Why have you brought me here ?"

"Ah ! You met your earlier incarnation, *Aoife*. Now *Banba*, the goddess of all things natural and Mother of Ireland, your second sister, would like to meet you. I am to take you to the place known as The Woodland."

He tells me that according to ancient Irish legend, Ireland was first called 'The Island of Banba of the Women'. *Banba* is one of the three goddesses of sovereignty.

I'm not sure about this, but I've got this far, so I decide to be brave. Opposite us is a woodland, thick with trees.

"Come," invites F*aoladh*. "There is a place in The Woodland where the river meets the trees. There is a curved lake which is formed from a horseshoe bend in the river where the main stream has cut across the narrow end and no longer flows around the loop of the bend. It forms a protective arc around those ancient trees."

"Oh, I understand. It's what we call a fairy ring. I learned its proper name in school. It's called an oxbow lake. "

He smiles again.

As we walk, there's something magical about this wood. We pass an old oak tree, gnarled by the years, its twisted branches heaven bound. They look like limbs dancing in the air. Perhaps they are shape-shifters too. Under our feet is what Da calls nature's compost. Leaves that are never swept away, but which generously give their nutrients to feed the soil in which the roots grow, so that the trees can stretch up and create the canopy above our heads. As we approach, we can hear the sound of the river. The gurgling water makes it seem as if it is laughing.

Faoladh points in the direction of the river. "Watch."
The centre of the water began to change. The river, which had been calm and serene, suddenly becomes a mass of liquid, whirling with a circular motion. As it continues, I see a cavity forming in the centre of the circle. The movement continues for several moments. As it speeds up it creates a whirlpool. As it reaches a crescendo, a living form rises up from the centre. It's a girl !

I keep my eyes on the figure as she rises up until she is hovering above the surface of the water. She floats across to the shore and stands in front of us.

I gasp. She's me. I am her ! Golden hair, blue eyes, a gown like floating chiffon. I notice she is not wet.

She holds out her arms to me. "Let me look at you, sister."

She gazes at me for a while. I am so surprised. I try and grasp what is happening.

She gives me a radiant smile. "*Aoife*. You are my soul-mate. Another version of me."

I must look bemused and puzzled.

"No harm will come to you here. We are woven together like sisters. With your other sister, we are triplets. Three in one."

I feel foolish. I don't know what to say.

"Usually you and I would not meet. We are in different worlds. You are 12, yes ?"

"I was, on my birthday."

"1st November ?"

"Yes."

"It's my day too." She grins reassuringly. "As you know, I am one of the goddesses of water. I am the guardian of the trees, the land, plants, animals, humans. All of Nature. My name means 'unploughed land'. I can mix a concoction which will give you natural wisdom for life. I am your protector. I am your sister and your guardian."

She sits on the shore and invites me to join her. I can't stop looking at this vision of myself. Like an identical twin.
When she speaks, I hear my own voice, but she sounds older and wiser. Probably, like F*aoladh*, she is immortal and has had many reincarnations over an expanse of time and space.

"I hear what you are thinking," she told me in a gentle voice. "You know from your reading that we understand that death is not a fixed state of being. It is just a stopping point to a change of time and place. Life goes on in all its forms in the Otherworld. When a soul dies in your world, it is reborn here, in the Otherworld. When a soul dies in the Otherworld, it is reborn in your world. You are my soul reborn in a physical state. As a human."

"I think I understand. It's a bit like going to Heaven or Hell. That's what we learn at school. Good and evil. Opposites."

"It's not quite the same. The Otherworld is one. Some beings here are partly bad and partly good. Like humans in a way. Not all of you are all good or all bad."

"That's true. Although, in our Catholic faith, we have an in-between place called Limbo or Purgatory. It's a kind of temporary punishment for those who are not all bad, but have done some bad deeds. The souls there are made ready for Heaven."

Aoife and F*aoladh* glance at one another. I can't work out what the look means, but I'm sure they are keeping something back that they don't want me to know. It unnerves me a bit. *Aoife* and *Faoladh* lead me back to the huge, ancient oak tree I had noticed on my way to the river.

Banba explains. "This oak is called *Bíle* (a sacred oak). Oak trees live for a long time. His longevity gives him wisdom. We often seek the advice of oak trees when making important decisions. You can also do this now as a True Believer."

Da has told me that this is one of the reasons why the Druids hold their gatherings in oak groves.

Banba continues. "*Bile* is *Danu*'s companion. *Danu* is the goddess who accompanies the souls on their journey from your world to the Otherworld. *Bile* then takes your dead and places them into the sacred river. *Bíle* has a special gate into the river. When the dead sink below the surface of the water, they are reborn."

This sounds amazing.

Bile – the sacred oak.

"You and I, *Aoife*, have our special day on 1st November. Your ancient Celtic people counted time as the night followed by the day. Their new year was at the festival of *Samhain*. That's the night of October 31st and the next day November 1st. So that's why, for True Believers, the New Year starts with the dark of night-time which marks the start of winter."

I do remember my parents said this was why my birthday was extra special. I also remember the name, *Danu*. All the gods of Ireland together are known as the *'Tuatha dé Danaan'*, which means the *'Tribe of Danu'*."

Danu.

Banba hears my thoughts. "*Danu* is a river goddess. It is believed by us, that *Danu* was one of the first visitors to planet Earth. It was a barren place. Dark and dry. *Danu* nourished the ground with all the water you have there. Rivers, lakes, seas. The Sun gods watched and liked what she was doing. They cast light on the planet. Together with the light, *Danu*'s watering began the life on earth. Just like planting seeds which need water to grow. At first tiny shoots, until a range of landscapes and creatures were created and began their lives. Including humans."

This is such an incredible story, I can hardly take it all in.

Banba continues. "To begin with, *Danu* only cast one, single seed on the ground. This seed grew into the oak we are standing under. It is why it is so tall and has so many legs and arms. *Danu* called the oak, *Bilé*. When *Danu* poured her water over *Bilé*, he drank greedily, for he was very thirsty. When he was fully grown, he produced two huge acorns. When these acorns fell to the ground, they became gods in their own right. The first acorn was a boy. He became what we call *The Dagda*, which means 'The Good God'...."

Dagda ! The god that Da was named after !

She continues, having heard my thought. "The second acorn was a girl. She was called *Brigid*, meaning 'The Exalted One'. "

Aunt *Brigid*. This is wonderful !

"*The Dagda* and *Brigid* studied one another in wonder. *Danu* spoke to them and gave them the task of becoming lovers and spreading the Children of *Danu*, the Mother Goddess, all over the Earth. They agreed to this because it was *Danu* whose divine waters had given them life."

I nod, any fear overcome by my concentration on this fascinating tale.

"The feeding of the Earth is what you in your heart should believe in and celebrate."

"I love the story," I tell her enthusiastically. "It's a bit like the Adam and Eve story in the Bible.

Neither of them respond.

I think about how my Aunt *Brigid* would also love to hear this. Maybe she knows it already ?

Banba adds, "*Bilé* will also be a guardian to you. His strength and wisdom will help to guide you through your life. He is The Tree of Life. His intricate network of branches represent how a family grows and expands throughout many generations. He also symbolises fertility. He always finds a way to keep growing, through spreading seeds or encouraging new saplings to grow to be lush and green, signifying vitality. You will learn and you will seek harmony with all."

Banba

I want to ask more, but *Banba* and F*aoladh* lead me back to the edge of the forest where F*aoladh* brought me when we left Earth.

I begin to feel tearful. "This has been wonderful, *Banba*, but I should go home," I tell her. "My Mam and Da will be very worried if I am not in bed when they get up this morning."

Banba puts her arm around my shoulder. "Fear not. F*aoladh* will take you back. You will arrive home at the same time as you left."

As she finishes speaking, she begins to fade away. I watch in amazement as she appears to melt into the dawn. She merges into a pink cloud, like a rose blossoming. I watch until the cloud fades away.

> *Thou are lovely, O Banba!*
> *Alone by the Western rocks!*
> *And the burning gold of thy locks,*
> *Down-streaming, a magickal tide,*
> *Over shoulder and radiant side,*
> *In waves in whose shadows were lost*
> *The lives of thy sacrificed host,*
> *And in gleaming of curling crests,*
> *Still lift, as of old, our breasts*
> *With thy rapture, O Banba!*

(extract from the poem, BANBA by poet Thomas Boyd - 1867–1927)

F*aoladh* takes my hand. We rise up into the approaching dawn and float away. Only moments later we descend like falling leaves. Drifting in the air like cascading parachutes.

"*Aoife. Aoife.*" I sleepily awake, hearing Mam's voice calling. "Hurry up, breakfast's nearly ready."

"Coming," I call.

I sit bolt upright, looking to see if *Faoladh* is still floating above the mantelpiece. No. Only my toys. I look round to reassure myself that I'm really in my bedroom. Wow ! What an incredible dream ! It seemed so real. I look down to check I'm wearing my nightie, not a beautiful silken gown.

Everything seems normal. I remember *Banba*'s words, "You will arrive home at the same time as you left."

I get washed and dressed. Was it really just a vivid dream ? I'm relieved to find myself at home, yet disappointed that I did not see more of the amazing world that my imagination has created.

....

I know that there are no real wolves in Ireland any more, but they were many. That would explain the large number of stories about them.

Da has given me a book to read about them. It seems they are complex creatures. They are often helpful, like my *Faoladh* and generally, benign. Some can be dangerous.

Luckily for me, it suggests that Irish wolves (or werewolves as they were known in mythological tales) were considered guardian spirits who protected children, wounded men, and those who were lost. These ideas are mainly from oral stories, rather than ancient writing. Interestingly, I have a classmate called Phelan. It says that his name comes from the word 'faol'. (wolf).

Da read to me the tale of 'The Werewolves of Ossory' which is an interesting one.

"A priest was travelling from Ulster to Meath with a friend. They took a rest and built a small fire. As they sat quietly, a wolf came up to them and started talking. As you can imagine, they were amazed !

'There are two of us wolves,' explained the wolf. 'We used to be human, a man and a woman, natives of a place known as Ossory. We were put under a curse by Natalis, a 6th century Irish monk and saint. It means that every seven years we have to throw off our human form and depart from the place we dwell and the people we know. We change from our bodies into the bodies of wolves. At the end of the seven years, if we survive, two other people from Ossory will be substituted in our place. Then, we can return to our home and our human form.'

The priest and his friend listened carefully.

The wolf continued. He explained that his female companion was dying. He had seen the priest approaching and begged him to give the woman the Last Rites. The priest followed the wolf to their lair, where he saw the female wolf, who is clearly about to die. He has doubts, however, about administering the holy sacrament to an animal. The wolf realises his concerns. He gently removes the female wolf's fur, revealing an old woman underneath.

The priest gives her the sacrament and she dies. The wolf then stays with the priest and his companion all night, talking round the fire."

Da pauses.

"The best part of this story is that the priest passed this story on to the bishop. He, in turn, sent it all the way to Pope Urban III. He lived from 1120 until 1187, so you can see how old the story is ."

I thought carefully about the story. The male wolf was obviously kind. He wanted his companion, maybe his wife, to die in a state of grace. The story is clearly based on a Christian idea.

Da explains that the story seems to be an unusual mix of beliefs or religions.

"The author of the book suggests that we often hear stories about shamans and other magicians sending forth their spirits, during which they lie as if dead or asleep."

Da smiles at me. Would you like another story ?"

I nod enthusiastically.

Da begins. "One such story is '*Laignach Faelad*' (Wolf Men of Tipperary).
"In a story called '*Coir Anmann*' it says that *Laignech Fáelad*, was an Earthly man who was also a shape-shifter. He used to shift into a *fáelad* (wolf-shape). He and his children would also shift ,whenever they liked, into the shapes of wolves."

Of course, I think of *Faoladh.*

"Unfortunately, they were not good wolves. They would catch and kill farm animals. The end of the story is not known, but the reader can guess !!"

"I don't like that story much !

"Ah well, the next story in the book is the most fascinating because you will recognise the names of the characters, *The Morrigan* and *Cúchulainn*. "

I have written about *Cúchulainn* in relation to my sister, *Aoife*. I also know that *The Morrigan* is well-known as a shape-shifter and a war-goddess. A wolf is just one of the many forms she can take.

"In an ancient story called '*Taín Bo CA*' , *The Morrigan* threatens the warrior, *Cúchulainn*, "I will drive the cattle on the ford to you, in the form of a grey wolf. Later, she fulfills her prophecy, when *Cúchulainn* was trying to protect the cattle of Ulster against *Queen Medb*'s raiders. She persuades the warrior, *Loch,* to fight him. She herself also attacked *Cúchulainn* three times. The first time, she shape-shifted into a hornless red cow with white ears. The second time, as a giant black eel, and finally, the third time as a grey-red wolf."

Da pauses. "I assume that the colours give us a clue that these animals were supernatural ! "

He continues. "Disguised as the she-wolf , *The Morrigan* attacks him, then drives the cattle towards him. *Cúchulainn throws* a stone from his sling, which hits her in the eye..... Again, frustratingly, the end of the story is missing.

"Oh," I say disappointedly. But I know many ancient stories were passed down orally and some, inevitably, were lost.

"One final story then," agrees Da. "It's called '*Fianna*'. It tells how a young man, Finn McCool, together with his warriors, comes to aid the *Fianna*. " He explains that a *fiann* was a group of landless young men and women, often aristocrats, who had not yet inherited property. There are many stories about these Irish groups. The main one *is Fiannaíocht ,* found in The Fenian Cycle.

"In the story, werewolves are the dogs of God. They go into Hell, which lies across the sea, three times a year to recover grain and cattle, stolen and taken there by sorcerers.

The food made from grain and the meat from the cattle is guarded by guards. They brutally beat anyone they catch, using broomsticks wrapped in horse hair. If the werewolves are unable to recover the grain, then there will be a poor harvest. He claims that werewolves go off into the woods, take off their clothing, and put on a wolf skin. They are transformed into wolves, and roam around in groups up to 30 strong, tearing to pieces any animal they come across, roasting it, and eating it. Occasionally, they also steal animals from farms for the same purpose."

"That sounds gruesome !"

Da told me that, in reality, the story was that the Fomorian king tried to starve the people of Ireland by levying such heavy taxes that they had no food. The other gods, led by Lugh, rose against him and defeated him and his clan.

"One more, please," I beg.

Da considers. "I think another story here is a bit of a variation of the story of Androcles and the Lion, which you've read. A man called Connor was searching for some missing cattle. He wandered so far that he got lost. He found a house and knocked on the door, but it turned out to be full of werewolves.

Connor was afraid. These were clearly Otherworldly creatures. However, it turned out that, some time before, he had removed a thorn that had got stuck in a baby werewolf's fur. Now, the werewolf was an adult, but he still recognised Connor. He remembered him with gratitude. The wolf invited Connor to have a meal with them. He did just that. Afterwards, he fell asleep. When he woke up in the morning everything was gone. Just like in fairy stories. The wolf that he had helped appeared and asked him to come outside. He had new cows for Connor. It suddenly struck Connor that this wolf was the pup he had helped."

I like the sound of that wolf. I can imagine *Faoladh* being that same wolf.

---

(8) Banba and Aoife in 'The Woodland'

"Books and talks and articles about Nature are little more than . . . dinner bells. Nothing can take the place of absolute contact, of seeing and feeding at God's table for oneself."

(John Muir – *1838-1914* - Scottish-American naturalist, author, environmental philosopher, botanist, zoologist, glaciologist)

Date: September 1966

It's a warm evening and I am reading, sitting in one of my favourite places by the river. It's Autumn, but the air is still warm. An autumnal breeze creates music. Gusts create a dramatic tempo and gentle zephyrs sweetly whisper a song. Amongst the trees of the forest behind me, *Bile*, the sacred Tree of Life, is the conductor of this orchestra playing under the canopy.

I sit watching the river closely. The forest and the river are keepers of poetry and song. They whisper sweet notes as they flow through the cascading water. As I watch I see salmon jumping upstream. I know a salmon's instinct to spawn kicks in around this time of year. This instinct causes them to swim back to the river where they were born in order to lay their eggs. It is possible to see ghostly salmon leaping here in the river as they try to catch invisible flies.

Banba has also told me that at times of impending danger, a herd of enchanted cows walk from the depths of the lake to graze on the meadows below the Castle.

No Earthly salmon or cows are to be found in the property !

As I leave my book and daydream, a mist forms on the surface of the river water. I know before I see her, it's *Banba*.

"Greetings sister." She speaks gently. "I see you embracing your land. It is possible to find something to love in all seasons. In this time when my Earth wears her warm hues. Her breeze is as a mother's kiss to the cheeks of all."

Banba continues and tells me that there are as many kinds of beauty as there are leaves in this autumnal forest.

Banba sighs happily. "The word 'beautiful' is a story of the innermost pages of your soul. It is the poetry of the soul that bonds you to all that is love. Just as starlight lights up the nightly heavens, the beauty of your heart is brightness to my heart."

I love the way *Banba* speaks to me. I want to remember her words when I write my own stories and tell of her visits in my journal.

Banba hovers closer." I have a story for you. I think you know the story of the princess and the frog."

I nod. Mam had read it to me and told me that the true moral of the story of 'The Frog Prince' is that in order to be loveable, a person must first be loved. Until the frog is kissed, he is ugly and despised. When he is kissed and loved, he becomes beautiful and loveable. Mam said that this story is an important piece of wisdom about how children should be taught to love all creatures whether ugly on the surface. Even those who may not appear beautiful on the outside, may well have beautiful souls.

My friend, Aisling and I used to dare one another to kiss a frog and see if it turned into a handsome prince. We did try, but the frogs didn't like it and neither did we. No handsome princes appeared !

Banba smiled at me indulgently. "In my story, there comes a time when a king, chieftain or ruler, has to embrace a beautiful, young goddess who has taken the guise of a very old woman. However, unbeknown to him, once he has kissed her, she will revert to her own image. Of course, then, he can fall in love with her and marry her. The idea is, that in completing this act, the king has revealed his respect for women, the givers of life through birth, life itself and death. What you call the natural cycle."

I consider this. It makes me realise how important physical features and first impressions are. Mam sometimes laughs and says, "the pastry may be plain, but what's inside the pie will be tasty !" She and Da always giggle together at this point.

An important, underlying aspect, which is key to this story, is the relationship between goddesses and human women. Mam has explained to me that the source of life is integral to the life of women for they are the bearers of life. Just as mothers like her protect their children and raise them, it would seem natural in times of greatest happiness, misery or pain, that human women would turn to their goddess protector to share joy, or for aid and support in a time of trouble. In my case, *Aoife* or *Banba* and in Mam's, *Macha*. In my family, Da has been a protector and teacher as well. He has been used to Mam being both independent and maternal at the same time. He has also played this role. He has the god *Dagda* to turn to when necessary.

Banba reads my thoughts. "Your parents have given you good guidance, for they are believers. Remember, you should always be a bright spirit in the dark, not exude a darkness of spirit. It's important to bring your light to others. Be generous in this. Seek the light with utter relentlessness. Walk with determination and thanks and joy. Never let bitterness enter your soul. Let it fall to the ground and tread it underfoot before it can reach your lips. Be proud in how you interact with others and never simply do selfish things with no consideration of consequences. Let your heart seek joy and learn to sing with courage and simple truth. Let the ways of love be your guide. Aim for a warm heart. "

She waits, hovering close, allowing me time to take in her wise words.

I concentrate hard, trying to fully understand what she says. It's very similar, though in different words, to what Mam and Da have taught me.

"It's not always easy," I reply. It's easy for us humans to lose our temper or be unkind. I do my best."

Banba reaches down and I feel her ghostly hand gently stroke my cheek.

"I know you will be one who heals and you will seek out others who heal to be your friends.

Although Mam is a nurse, I am very squeamish about blood. I must have made a face.

Banba laughs, a kind of giggle, like birdsong. "I mean a spiritual healer, a comforter."

Now, I'm the one who laughs.

Banba adds, "remember to always ask, why? Always try to see how ideas can be combined - often things that seem incompatible are two parts of the same puzzle. Learn compromise. Learn to be an embodiment of kindness, actively rejecting opportunities to do anyone else harm with your voice or your action. Do this, and you will feel your own spirit developing, growing stronger. You are moving from child to adult , where your true self is waiting within to be revealed."

I'm keen to ask more questions, but *Banba* is already fading. From the cushion of cloud she creates, the mist is taken into the trees and plants, moistening the air and feeding the river. I look up and feel a delicate dampness resting itself on my face.

It's getting late. I gather up my book and set off for home with a light heart. The trees rustle, as if waving. I wave back.

---

(9) Macha Ryan (Mam) — A True Believer

Date: 1967

After my first visit from *Aoife*, I wasn't sure whether to confide in Mam and Da. Neither of them said anything, but somehow they knew. It was unspoken between us, but I knew they understood.

My Mam was born in Blarney. She is one of 12 children ! Mam is the third eldest. I have her colouring of golden hair and blue eyes. She met my Da in 1949. She says it was love at first sight. Macha McSweeney became Macha Ryan !

Mam's spiritual sister is *Macha*, often known as the horse goddess and Mam has been around horses all her life. My granddad was a blacksmith. In Irish mythology, the god *Goibniu* was the metalsmith of the *Tuatha Dé Danann*. He is also associated with hospitality. That certainly sounds like my granddad who loves a drink or two !

We have a field at the bottom of our garden where Mam's horse, also called *Macha*, loves to run.

Mam's horse, Macha.

Macha is a handsome palomino stallion. He has a bright, rich golden body with white mane and tail. Palomino horses like him are known for their colouring which flashes and glimmers in the sun. Mam says that Palominos need higher levels of daily care because of their fast metabolism and energy needs, He's hot-blooded and passionate. That said, he adores Mam and they are certainly matched in temperament !

Mam has told me the story of Palominos. Apparently, during her reign in the Middle Ages, Queen Ysabella de Bourbon of Spain kept 100 'pale palomino' Spanish horses as the chosen mounts for Royalty and Nobility only. Other people were forbidden from owning and riding them. Even today these pale palomino horses are called 'Isabellas' in Spain and Europe.

Mam explained, "in 1519 Queen Isabella financed an exploratory trip to the 'New World', which is now Mexico. So enchanted was she with her 'Golden Horses', that she sent a stallion and five mares on that expedition to breed and spread across new lands discovered by Spanish explorers. These original Spanish horses bred and spread all the way up into North America. In fact, those original horses have formed the basis of all native American stock today."

Mum listens indulgently as I tell her about palominos on American television. "I love Mr. Ed, the Talking Horse. He is in an American TV series. He's a talking palomino. His real name is Bamboo Harvester .

Mr.Ed.

My favourite palomino is Trigger who belongs to Roy Rogers, my favourite television cowboy. Trigger's real name is Golden Cloud.

Trigger and Roy Rogers with fellow actress Lynne Roberts.

"Where did the name 'palomino originally come from ?" I ask Mam.

She pauses. "The Arabic word 'izbah', which translates to 'pale' or 'light', or even 'lion-coloured', was often applied to ermine furs that were traded from Arabia to Europe in Elizabethan times, so it may have been applied to horses with that colouring."

Mam laughs to herself as she searches her own memory. She tells me that she learned to ride as a toddler on a pony. By her teens, she was a skilled rider and took place in many competitions. She also tried bareback riding which was common in this area for those who couldn't afford saddles and used their mounts as work horses as well.

I lean forward on my seat, keen to know more.

"Even before the Spanish connection, we don't know precisely where the first palominos emerged in this world. Myths and legends from the great ancient empires of Rome, Greece, Persia, Mongolia, China and Japan all feature images and stories of golden horses. The immortal Xanthus, a word meaning 'golden', pulled the chariot of Achilles in Homer's Iliad and was gifted speech by the gods. Records have survived from Imperial China of horses featuring the palomino colouration, wearing tack which was coloured the distinctive blue reserved for Chinese royalty."

"So they have a history of being revered and important ?"

"Indeed. The Crusades saw many palominos transferred to European soil. One famous example is that of the general Saladin in the 12th century. He was the Sultan of Egypt and Syria. He was defeated by the Europeans in battle in the wars we know as The Crusades. King Richard 1 of England….."

"Richard the Lionheart ?" I interrupt.

"That's right. You probably know that King Richard was famous for fighting his Muslim enemies. He led armies of Christians in battles against Saladin and his armies."

"We've learnt about him in school. The nuns told us that the Muslims were pagans and the Christians had to defend themselves against them."

Mam gives me one of her enigmatic smiles. There's obviously more to it than that, but she doesn't like to contradict my teachers.

"Here's a question," says Mam. "What is the link between Saladin, Richard the Lionheart and a golden horse ?"

I shrug my shoulders, but I'm keen to hear the answer. I love these stories. It brings Mam and I closer and I learn more than I ever do in school. I don't let on though.

Mam takes a breath and begins.

"Well now, in the 12th century, Saladin, Sultan of Eygpt and Syria, who lived from 1137 until 1193, had a number of Battles with King Richard 1 of England – as you said, known as The Lionheart. Richard was born in 1157 and died in 1199. During his life, he went on many long journeys to fight enemies of Christianity in what we call The Crusades. He spent a lot of time out of England.

Historians say that Saladin's relationship with Richard appears to have been one of chivalrous mutual respect as well as military rivalry. Richard even praised Saladin as being the greatest and most powerful leader in the Islamic world, and Saladin in turn stated that there was no more honourable Christian lord than Richard.

Richard and Saladin never actually met each other face to face, even though their armies clashed several times during the course of the Third Crusade. However, the story of the Third Crusade has been recounted as a personal duel between the two leaders.

Richard had fought his way into English legend as leader of the Third Crusade (1189- 92). So had Saladin to his own people. The two men were said to be well matched in skill. They had high regard for each other and fought nobly. However, the major difference between the two was that Saladin himself did not engage in combat, while Richard lived for it and was known as a ferocious fighter."

"I wonder why Saladin didn't fight himself ?"

"I suppose it was the culture of the time. Maybe he was like a kind of god to his people, so he wouldn't fight ordinary men."

Mam continues.

"Anyway, at the Battle of Jaffa, Saladin had to call for reinforcements . He raised around 20,000 soldiers. In the meantime, Richard had lost a lot of men in the battle, even though he'd managed to break into the city of Jaffa. He decided to lead his small force out from behind Jaffa's walls. He placed his knights and men-at-arms in a single line, with each man kneeling on one knee and thrusting the butt of his spear or lance into the sand to make a kind of hedge as a barrier of steel. Then, between and behind these men he placed his crossbowmen in pairs, one to fire and one to reload, so as to achieve the highest rate of fire."

Mam pauses, giving me time to take all this in.

"The Muslim army arrived and they attacked in waves. However, the Crusaders' storm of crossbow bolts easily penetrated the Muslims' light armour, killing both men and beasts. Finally, Saladin's troops turned away, unwilling to charge into the Crusaders' hedge of steel."

"I'm not surprised."

"Richard then charged with 15 mounted knights. No enemy was safe within his reach, and twice he rescued his own knights who had fallen from their horses."

Mam stops for a moment and then continues. "The battle then paused for a short time. Richard continued fighting even though he was on foot after his only warhorse had been killed. Then, an amazing thing happened. Saladin, seeing his enemy's predicament and being so impressed with Richard's bravery, declared that such a courageous man should not fight without a mount. He sent Richard two splendid warhorses. They were what we call 'Palomino' horses. They were unknown to Europeans at that time."

I try to imagine Richard and his men's surprise when they see these wonderful horses.

King Richard with Saladin's gift of two palomino stallions

At the time of Saladin and Richard, they weren't known as palominos. The Muslim word for them was more likely to have derived from the Arabic word 'izbah' which means pale or light or even lion-coloured."

"Throughout history there have been reports of men from the East riding golden horses during battles. They were much admired by Europeans both military and civilian, although there was a fear that these horses could come from the 'Otherworld'. For example, Pegasus, the winged flying horse in Greek mythology, had a golden coat."

I nod enthusiastically. "I know the story of Pegasus. I hadn't thought of him as connected with palominos."

Mam suggests that after The Crusades, it was likely that these horses could have been collected from battlefields as spoils of war. They would have been taken back to different European countries. Over centuries, they would have been bred and it's why we have them today.

Mam also explains that 'Palomino' is a Spanish word meaning 'dove-like', which clearly refers to the paleness of their coats. She tells me that the name for such horses in Europe may have originated with a Spanish man called Juan de Palomino. He was a conquistador, known for riding a golden stallion known as a 'palomino'.

Mam pauses.

"As well as the two stallions given to Richard the Lionheart by the Sultan Saladin as a gift, many crusaders spoke of other golden horses which they saw being ridden by their enemies. It's likely that a number of these horses were returned with them to their homelands as spoils of war. They most likely were bred and the eye-catching colouring passed on into the bloodlines of European horses. That's how, even after thousands of years, the human fascination with horses of gold remains as steadfast as ever."

Da has been reading all this time, although I noticed he's been earwigging from time to time as Mam tells her tale. I notice as he searches the book shelf.

"Ah, here it is," he declares. "I remember a poem I read about the golden horses. Sadly, it's anonymous, but it shows the true nature of palominos. It's called 'The Andalusian', which is after an area of Spain. He clears his throat and begins to read aloud.

> *"His stance is proud*
> *His heart is pure*
> *His loyalty unbound*
> *And when he runs, his hoofbeat echo*
> *Thunders noble sound*
> *His swiftness challenges the wind*
> *In untamed Majesty*
> *His spirit ever riderless*
> *His soul forever free..."*

I sigh happily. I love these stories. Horses are incredible creatures. We're lucky to have them.

---

(10) Epona — Horse and Goddess

Date: 1968

I have been riding since I was small. Not quite a toddler, but I've had lessons at the local riding stables since I was about 5. Now, I have my own horse, *Epona*. Named after a Celtic goddess, she made her first appearance on my 14th birthday. Of course, she's a palomino and daughter of *Macha*, Mam's horse. She is a pale, mysterious steed and I love her dearly.

I have spent a lot of time reading about the goddess *Epona*. *She is* the patron of horses and also of donkeys and mules. The word 'epo' is the Gaulish equivalent of the Latin 'equus', meaning horse. In Irish, a horse is called a '*capall*' and equine is '*eachaí*'.

The majority of inscriptions and images bearing *Epona*'s name have been found in the area once known as Gaul, Germany, and the Danube countries. Some created in Roman times have been found on the site of the barracks of the 'Equites Singulares', an imperial bodyguard made up of foreign troops.

The cult of worshipping the goddess *Epona* does not appear to have been introduced into Rome before Imperial times, when she was often called *Augusta* and invoked on behalf of the Emperor and the Imperial household. The Romans used to place the image of *Epona/Augusta*, which was crowned with flowers on festive occasions, in a sort of shrine in the centre of the architrave of the stable. In art she is generally represented seated, with her hand placed on the head of the accompanying horse or donkey.

Epona

"It was set up for you, Sacred Mother.
It was set out for you, Atanta.
This sacrificial animal was purchased for you, horse goddess, Eponina.
So that it may satisfy, horse goddess Potia; we pay you, Atanta, so that you are satisfied; we dedicate it to you.
By this sacrificial animal, swift Ipona, with a filly, goddess Epotia
for a propitious lustration they bind you, Catona of battle, with a filly, for the cleansing of riding horses
which they cleanse for you, Dibonia.
This swift mare, this cauldron, this smithwork, beside fat and this cauldron."

This lovely dedication to *Epona* was found in 1887 at Rom in the Deux-Sevres area of France. It was inscribed on a thin lead plate and written in Latin. It's thought to date from the first century BC. It has been suggested by a historical translator that it is a very close example to a Vedic hymn to Indra. The Vedas are a large body of religious texts from ancient India. They date from as long ago as 1500–1200 BC.

Epona is also known as the Great Mare. She is, first and foremost, a Goddess of Horses associated with the Gauls and Celts. Because of the oral nature of many legends, in this case, there's not too much about *Epona*. However, the Gauls and others did leave a rich legacy of inscriptions and monuments and it is from this that most of the evidence for *Epona* comes.

Da searched for me in the university library. He found one story related to *Epona*'s origin that has survived. There was a Greek writer called Agesilaos. He wrote that *Epona* was born through a love affair between a mare and a man called Phoulonios Stellos. This man preferred horses to women ! The mare gave birth to a beautiful and lively daughter whom she named *Epona*. This child became the Goddess of Horses.

I know that part of the Otherworld's and Celtic cultures is that the giving of a name is vitally important to that being's future. The naming of *Epona* by her mother implies that the mare had a divine nature herself. *Epona* was therefore a reincarnation of an earlier Horse Goddess.

One thing I love the idea of is that small images of *Epona* have been found in stables and barns all over Europe. A niche would be cut in the walls and a little statue of *Epona* placed there so that it could be used as a shrine. Sometimes it would have a garland of roses over it or, occasionally, created with a mare's head with a human body. *Epona* is occasionally depicted in a human form with a foal, or feeding foals. This suggests a maternal role for her, like many other goddesses. In most images, *Epona* is portrayed as a woman either sitting on, or surrounded by, horses.

She is also often portrayed with a Cornucopia. In ancient times, the cornucopia, (two words from Latin 'cornu' and 'copia'), also called 'the horn of plenty', was a symbol of abundance and nourishment. Commonly it was a large horn-shaped container overflowing with produce, flowers, fruit and nuts.

A cornucopia

It's a symbol of the land and of fertility. *Epona* has also been seen carrying keys. This is showing off one of her roles in the Otherworld. She is often accompanied by birds, which, in this case, are symbols of happiness.

The Uffington White Horse in England is thought to be one of the largest remaining monuments to *Epona* in the British Isles. Experts are not sure whether is was carved by those who worshiped *Epona*. Some of us are sure though !

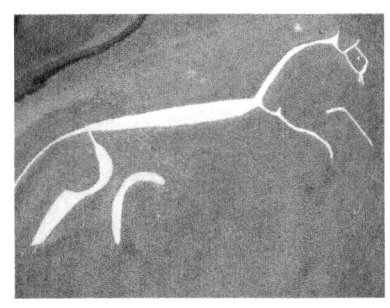

The Uffington White Horse

The Uffington White Horse is a prehistoric hill figure. It's 360 feet long and formed from deep trenches filled with crushed white chalk. The figure is situated on the upper slopes of White Horse Hill in the South of England.

Epona is known to be one of a very few Gaulish and Celtic deities whose names were spread to the rest of the Roman Empire. This seems to have happened because Roman cavalry units stationed in Gaul came to admire and follow her and ultimately adopted her as their Patroness. The Gauls were known as superb horsemen. The Romans took the cult of *Epona* with them to Rome where she was given her own feast day on the 18 December. *Epona* is recognised as being high in the status of goddesses. Horse symbolism is a theme of sovereignty.

There are other deities that have the horse as one of their sacred animals but few, if any, with as strong a link to the land as *Epona* seems to have.

Since having my horse, I have also discovered that *Epona* is the patroness of all journeys, whether physical, mental, emotional and spiritual. Alongside *Aoife* and *Banba*, I feel her presence when I am riding. She is my spiritual mother, my equine sister and my friend when my Epona and I are exploring the countryside. Especially then, I feel her presence beside me keeping me safe. As my riding skills improve, I find her giving me strength for each new challenge.

Mam has started to teach me to ride bareback. Riding a horse bareback is a great way to develop your muscles and improve your balance.

Mam says, "In the winter, it's easier and less cumbersome if you only have a short time for a quick ride around the paddock. "

I have found already that riding bareback also helps me to have a more instinctive feel for how Epona moves. It's a wonderful feeling when I feel her muscles working beneath me. It's like being one with her.

Today Mam is helping me to prepare Epona for a bareback riding session. It definitely helps that Epona and I have a close understanding how each of us think and move.

Mam advises me, " it's important to make sure that Epona is calm and at ease before you begin."

I feel quite confident about this. *Epona* has a healthy back which is comfortable for me to ride bareback and she and I have that deep bond of trust between us.

Mam knows this and she knows I can ride well.

Mam instructs, "before you begin, I want you to demonstrate the halt, turning, walk, the sitting trot, posting trot, and the canter/lope in the saddle, both with and without stirrups. Once I'm sure you've mastered these moves, we can begin training."

I know that a saddle helps distribute a rider's weight across a horse's back. Without it, my weight will rest in a smaller spot. I have practised this as well. Epona is great because, just like her goddess namesake, I believe she can think in both woman and equine form, so she understands each.

Because I've only just started bareback riding, Mam gets me to practise for a short time each day. I'm only too pleased to do this. She has explained that a good time to practise riding bareback is after a ride. Epona will be warmed up and I can remove the saddle and ride bareback for a short time.

Mam continues. "Don't forget, mounting any horse bareback is a skill to be learned. You won't have the stirrups to use to mount up, so you need to find a mounting block."

That's important for me to learn, because at the moment, Mam can just give me a leg up !

"You can use a handy fence rail to mount up, " advises Mam, "but it's sometimes difficult to get your horse lined up and standing still while you balance precariously on the fence like a tightrope walker !"

I laugh.

Mam grins. "The other reminder is not to line *Epona* up along something where she could get a bridle strap or rein tangled . It's essential to keep her as near as possible to the mounting spot. If she's not lined up and fully ready, it's easy for you to fall. I I only made this mistake once," admits Mam and it was my own fault."

I am learning to watch for *Epona*'s cues and only mount when she is not moving and ready for me.

Mam has also explained that it's critical to maintain a comfortable position.

"Once you're up, get comfortable and make sure Epona is comfortable too. Remember, a good position is the same as in the saddle. You want bareback riding to improve your riding overall, not become a way to develop new bad habits !"

I nod seriously, taking in all this advice.

She watches closely. "Once you're up, she calls, "be aware of the alignment of your ear, shoulder, hip, and heel. Aim to be light in your seat so you aren't a dead weight on her back."

She waits until she's satisfied with what I've done.

"Now, Aoife, I'm going to lead you."

Mam begins to lead Epona at a walk. She gets her to walk forward, turn, halt, and back-up.

This is great. It gets me and Epona, used to the sensation. As soon as Mam is happy with the trials, she leaves me waiting while she mounts Macha. She walks Macha alongside Epona.

"Now, when you and Epona are feeling secure, take up the reins and try to start, steer, and stop. I'm coming along for security."

After a time, Mam gets us to repeat the procedure while Epona is moving at both a sitting and 'posting' trot.

Mam taught me posting. It's when you rise up out of the saddle seat for every other stride of the horse's forelegs. This helps to smooth out the jolts that you would encounter if you just sat still in the saddle. It certainly makes riding the trot much more comfortable for me and Epona !

"You should practise being able to post without stirrups or a saddle," Mam calls.

We practise several times. Epona and I feel quite relaxed at the end.

"We'll have another go next time and then move on," Mam says. "No point in rushing things."

We lead our horses back towards the pasture. Horseback riding is the closest I have ever come to dreaming while being perfectly awake. It's such a strong sensation that being with Epona is my kind of heaven. Once I'm up on her back, we are as one.

Macha and Epona, together with Mam and I, amble through the petal-freckled paths of Spring. We are carried along the field edges and down to the clear waters of the gurgling river where the horses can drink their fill. Mam and I sit under the shade of a tree. Mam produces from nowhere a flask and two beakers. She pours the silver liquid. We drink in silence, absorbing the scene. I let the sharp, yet sweet, flavour of home-made lemonade slide down my throat.

Reluctantly, we leave for home. Back on horseback, we feel connected to the earth by hoof. We are indeed indebted to the horses that carry us with such loving care. They are family too. They love to run as much as us and put their hearts into the mission as much as we do. Four hearts make their way through the sparkling sunshine. Each horse and its human rider acting as one . To see the world from horseback is a privilege, one for which we owe thanks to our four-footed friends.

....

Recently, just after my 14th birthday, Mam and I were talking about women's rights. Mam gave me an example of a mythological story which shows how the treatment and perception of women has changed over time. In one particular incarnation, *Macha* was married.

The tale demonstrates how the king (male) at this point in time has power over the goddess (female).

It was a dark, chilly evening. The heavens were black. The stars were invisible, tucked up snug in the dark. Mam and I sat in front of a peat fire. I find that the fireside brings the kind of glow that resonates with my heart and makes it warm. Mam and I together, close and cosy.

Mam smiled at me as she began. The storyteller uplifting the heart of the listener, I thought.

" Long ago, *Macha* was a revered and powerful goddess. She could appear in many guises, particularly as a horse. As this elegant steed, she could run like the wind and had bravery enough to fill the verses of many a minstrel's ballad. Her fame spread far and wide, both on Earth and in the Otherworld for centuries and millenia to come...."

She paused while I snuggled down in my fireside chair. We all love the fireside, the hearth, the shelter of the golden light of candles on nights like this. Da reckons that it's heaven right here on Earth !

Mam continues. "In what we on Earth would call the Medieval Period, *Macha* married *Crunnchua mac Angnoman,* a rich widower from Ulster in Ireland. All was well until one day, *Crunnchua* wished to go to the annual assembly of the Ulstermen. *Macha* pleaded with him not to go. She foresaw the consequences. However, *Crunnchua* ignored her advice and insisted on going.

Whilst at the assembly, *Crunnchua* watched a horse race. Those Ulstermen with him, including the King himself, declared that none could run faster than these horses.

Now, *Crunnchua* believed that his wife could outrun these horses with no problem and he decided to challenge the declaration. The King was angered by *Crunnchua*'s arrogance and insisted that *Crunnchua* should bring *Macha* to race against them if he was so confident about her ability.

Macha reluctantly came, but she begged the king not to make her race as she was pregnant. She was afraid of the consequences for the unborn child. She looked at the crowd of men and pleaded with them.

'Help me, for a mother bore each of you. Give me, oh, King, but a short delay until I am delivered.'

"Her request was refused by the King," Mam told me angrily.

"That's awful," I grumbled.

"You're right," agreed Mam. "You see, in stories of the Celtic pre-Christian era, it would have been the King's responsibility to allow the creativity of women to continue and thrive. Kings were expected to promise that no woman would die in child birth. Food should grow in plenty to feed the children and keep them healthy. These promises were related to the needs and concerns of women. If a King could not be seen to take care of the cultural and fertility needs of the clan, symbolised by these women's activities, he would be overthrown. However, in this instance, the King violated the needs of a pregnant woman. Yet, instead of being overthrown, he is allowed to continue his reign with no apparent resistance from his people."

We both sit quietly, contemplating the change in behaviour of that particular King.

Mam added, "of course, this portrayal of *Macha* is actually the last one in the three major cycles of the Ulster stories. In the first story, she is a brilliant, strong mother-goddess. In the second she is a helpless, but wise wife. In the third she is relegated to an existence of shame and forced to endanger her life-giving gifts."

We sit quietly, digesting the meaning of the story.

Mam continued. "This is how the presentation of *Macha* in stories has changed over time. She has latterly become traditionally associated with the three war-goddess spiral, joining in sisterhood to form a trio with *Badb* and *Morrigan*. The concept of the brave and chivalrous warrior goddess appears to have been transformed as a result of the change in Celtic society to one of greater violence...." Mam hesitated. "Paradoxically, running parallel with the onset of Christianity."

She made the sign of the cross as if to let God know she's sorry for this blasphemy.

I bit my tongue and said nothing.

Mam continued to explain how the perception of *Macha* had changed.

"*Macha*"s nature has been reconstructed, making her into a malign type of warrior-goddess. Sadly, this demonstrates the way in which the status of women in society was declining at that period in history. Of course, it didn't happen overnight. As Celtic societies moved towards fighting and war, the emphasis was focussed on death and bloodlust, rather than on the creation of life and respect for death."

I was puzzled. "But isn't creation of life and respect for death a Christian idea ?"

Mam emphasised again how, within this change, the decline of goddess deities ran parallel with the influence of Christian clerics.

"Earthly men began to feel threatened by women. They saw women as competitors. Their patriarchal system of beliefs, that is that the man was head of the household and inheritance ran down through the male heirs, was in direct contrast to the worship of female deities. Priests and monks were male so they wanted to take control and undermine the power of the goddesses. You have seen this for yourself in stories from myth and legend. Often this showed itself in violent ways in both the stories and here in the Earthly world. Women were treated badly and strong women and those such as healers and midwives were said to be in league with the devil."

"Like the women who were called witches ?"

"That's right."

"And women still can't be priests ?"

"Not in the Catholic faith," answered Mam apologetically.

There's a lot for me to read about and get to understand better. I know Mam is a True Believer, but I am beginning to realise there is a conflict between her spiritual relationship with those from The Otherworld and her desire to believe in a Christian God. It's a difficult balancing act.

---

(11) Dagda Ryan (Da) - A True Believer

Druids

Date 1966

Da's god is The *Dagda* – In Irish: An *Dagda*. He's an important god in Irish mythology. One of the *Tuatha Dé Danann*. The *Dagda* is a father-figure, king, and Druid. He is associated with fertility, agriculture, manliness and strength, as well as magic, Druidism and wisdom.

Dagda

Mam and I like this image of The Dagda. I think it looks jolly. Mam teases him about the size of the stomach !

My Da is not a Catholic. In fact the traditions of his family have more to do with Irish Druidism. These wise people act as priests, teachers, and judges. He has told me that the earliest known records of the Druids come from the 3rd century BC. Their name comes from a Celtic word meaning 'knower of the oak tree.' A link with *Bile* ? Very little is known for certain about early Druids, who kept no written records of their own.

Da has told me that these days, the word Druid conjures up thoughts of magic, wizardry, and spiritualism. Non-believers think it's all what Da calls "jiggery-pokery".

True Believers in the Otherworld also know the links between Earthly Druids and Supernatural Beings. In the ancient times Druids were extremely important to the ancient Celtic people.

They made up the higher echelons of Celtic society. They were well educated and well-read. Druids were often poets, doctors, and spiritual leaders. Their job as spiritual leaders has endured for thousands of years and will continue into infinity. They had an air of mystery about them, which makes me very interested in what Da tells me and reads to me. I'm going to write about them from the beginning.

Da has explained how ancient the Druid spiritual tradition really is. The earliest evidence is from 25,000 years ago. It's found in caves such as the Pinhole caves in Derbyshire in England, the Chauvet or Lascaux caves in France, and the Altamira in Spain, which feature paintings of wild animals on their walls.

I can see how Da, who's such a kind and open person, likes Druidism and relates to its openness. One of its most striking characteristics is the degree to which it is free of fixed set of beliefs or practices. Unlike the Catholic church, I think ! But that's just my opinion. It manages to offer people a spiritual path and a way of being and behaving in the world that avoids many of the problems of what I'd call established religions. Druids are tolerant and open-minded. They don't have the equivalent of a bible and there is no single, rigid, set of beliefs amongst Druids. Despite this, there are lots of ideas and beliefs that most Druids hold in common. I do wonder though how, in some respects, Mam and Da don't end up crossing swords as their beliefs do sometimes contradict each other. I guess that's what being respectful of other people's views is all about.

Da tells me that Druids are open-minded about the number of gods and goddesses there might be. "In fact," he says, "none of us has the monopoly on truth and, anyway diversity is both healthy and natural !"

I smile. I like this approach to life.

Da has taken me to Druid gatherings since I was small. These are designed to bring together people who have widely varying views about deities, or no particular view. These get-togethers have a happy, relaxed atmosphere. People participate in ceremonies together, celebrate the seasons, and enjoy each others' company .

Like other things in both the Earthly and Other worlds, nature forms such an important focus. All Druids sense Nature as being divine or sacred.

"Think of a huge spider's web," Da told me. "Every part of nature is sensed as part of what we could call 'The Great Web of Life'. No beings or creatures have more control or ownership of it than another. "

I consider this. "So, it's not like some religions (I don't mention Catholic !) where one God is supreme over everyone else ?"

"That's right," encourages Da. "There is no 'Fat Controller', like in Thomas the Tank Engine' ! We just see humankind as one part of the wider family of life."

Da pats his own tubby tummy and makes me laugh.

The Fat Controller from 'The Railway' series by Reverend W. Awdry.

What Da explains about links with the Otherworld does tie in with the family's communication with our Otherworldly sisters and brother.

"Although Druids love Nature, and we draw inspiration and spiritual nourishment from it, of course, we also believe that our Earthly world isn't the only one that exists. A cornerstone of Druid belief is in the existence of the Otherworld." He stops and smiles at me reassuringly. "As you know, Aoife, and have experienced, it's a realm or likely more than one, which exists beyond the reach of the physical senses, but which are nevertheless real."

"But there are people who don't agree. I have to keep quiet at school in front of the nuns and only some of the girls are Believers, like us."

Da nods sympathetically. "Most non-believers think of the Otherworld as either heaven or hell…and maybe even limbo. We have the same idea that it's the place we travel to when we die. But, the difference is we know that we can also visit it during our lifetime. Sometimes it comes to us in dreams. Other times we go on a kind of journey."

"It's hard to explain."

"You're right. To start with it doesn't seem so different. All religions or belief systems, hold the view that another reality exists beyond our physical, Earthly world. That seems simple…."

I laugh.

"OK – maybe not ! But it's easier for us because we have had this wonderful opportunity to experience the Otherworld and its beings. We take it for granted. Druid funerals try to focus on the idea that the soul is experiencing a time of birth, even though we are experiencing that as their death to us."

It's a lot to take in.

"Let's give our brains a rest," grins Da. "I fancy a cuppa and one of those nice scones Mam cooked this morning."

Arm in arm we head to the kitchen.

....

Another time, on the last Midwinter's Day. Da tells me a story. We are sitting in my bedroom which faces west. It's the end of the day.

"Did you know ?", Da begins, the winter solstice, which is also called the Hiemal (Hibernal) Solstice, occurs when either of Earth's poles reaches its maximum tilt away from the Sun. This happens twice yearly, once in each hemisphere....."

"We learnt at school that it's before Christmas, but the day can vary a little depending on the exact time and date of the tilt."

"That's right. Winter sunsets are created by *Áine*, the Irish goddess of summer. She is associated with midsummer and the sun. She's sometimes represented by a stunning red mare. We miss the sight of the sun in winter, so *Aine* comes to the sky and warms it. Like you, dancing to that pop music you like to keep warm ! Da grins.

I stick out my tongue at him.

Da continues. "As you know, the Celtic calendar is a compilation of pre-Christian Celtic systems of timekeeping. It's used by Celtic countries to define the beginning and length of the day, the week, the month, the seasons, quarter days, and festivals."

I nod because I know about this from previous chats with Da.

In December, here in the Northern hemisphere, the date also marks the 24-hour period with the fewest daylight hours of the year. That is why it's known as the shortest day of the year, or the longest night of the year.

Midwinter is also known as Yuletide. In modern Druid traditions, we call it *Alban Arthan*. It's been recognised as a significant turning point in the yearly cycle since the late Stone Age. ... Traditionally, this is the most important time of celebration."

"And, of course, on 25th December, it's a Christian day for celebrating the birth of Jesus Christ."

"Not forgetting Christmas presents as well !"

Da and I laugh together.

I like the mix of the festivals and celebrations. It merges together the two different paths of Christianity and paganism and helps me to grasp the best of both. It doesn't have to be either / or.

───────────────────────────

(12) Aoife Ryan Muses

2021

Re-reading some of the sections of my journal from so long ago is like reading it for the first time and yet it all quickly becomes clear when my memory gets a nudge.

The entry about Mam and *Macha* and the ideas that arose from it, makes me think of how things have moved on over those 54 years !

As I know, once Christianity began to spread, God, the father, gradually took the place of female deities. Male priests and vicars were God's representatives and women were cut out of these positions of care and authority.

Even in these modern times, the Church of England only first allowed the ordination of women to priesthood in 1992, with ordinations not commencing until 1994.

Among the most vocal, still current, controversies in the Catholic Church has been the question of the ordination of women. As more Protestant denominations have begun ordaining women, the Catholic Church's teaching on the all-male priesthood has come under attack. There are those who claim that the ordination of women is simply a matter of justice, and the lack of such ordination is proof that the Catholic Church does not value women.

The Church, however, still stamps its foot and refuses change. So, I'm thinking of female deities, especially in the context of those I have been in direct contact with and their important position in societies, both ancient and modern.

I have asked a young priest I know, Father Morley, the question – "why can't women be priests ?"

He explained that "The Church argues that the answer to the question is simple. The New Testament priesthood is the priesthood of Christ himself. Christ was a man, therefore, *'quod erat demonstrandum' !"*

His eyes twinkled, but I decided to push the matter further.

"Of course Christ was a man. I'm giving you the benefit of the doubt regarding whether he really existed. But, surely, a woman can act in the person of Christ as well as a man can ?"

Father Morley considered my point. "Well now, The Church argues that the ordination of men is an unbroken tradition that goes back not only to the Apostles but to Christ himself. "

Cheekily I responded, "but surely traditions are like pie crusts, sure to be broken ?"

He hesitated.

I knew he had to be careful and give me a considered response.

"I'm afraid the Catholic Church insists its views are irreducible. Men and women, by their natures, are suited to different, yet complementary, roles and functions ! "

"Oh, really ?"

He grinned, but made it clear he wouldn't commit himself further.

As a child brought up in Ireland, I was always taken by Mam to Mass every Sunday. I also suffered attendance at a girls' Catholic convent school run by nuns. Not so much the religion, as the nuns themselves. They seemed so old and staid when I was young. I must admit, even now, I find The Otherworld and all it offers more challenging and exciting. Yet, I don't completely reject Christianity. The best of both is perhaps the most satisfactory compromise.

The philosophy underpinning my own experience of education was based on the sole belief that everything was 'sinful'. That certainly included pop music. I remember a friend and I were told that singing 'She Loves You' by The Beatles was tantamount to insulting both God and Christ and would certainly end in certain banishment to hell when we died. However, according to Sister Hosanna, our music teacher, there was a way to redeem ourselves. That was to spend our lunch hour missing out on food and spending the time repeatedly singing 'Ave Maria'.

I later suspected, although Mam would never have admitted it, that she had taken me to Mass and sent me to a Catholic school as a kind of insurance policy against the possibility that a paternal God and his apparently sexist son, Jesus Christ, might just exist in the form our local priest, Father O'Donnelly. He would insist upon sentencing me, and her, to eternal damnation if we didn't attend services !

There is, of course, more recently, a suggestion that would have no doubt incurred a heart attack in poor old Father O'Donnelly. Namely that one of Christ's disciples may have been a woman. None other than Mary Magdalene !

It's interesting that this woman is portrayed by the Catholic Church as a 'fallen woman', a prostitute, therefore lacking any status in the society of her time. Just as a personal aside, it is interesting also that there were 12 apostles. Could this be a continuation of the ancient Celtic belief in the importance of the number 3 and its multiples in terms of fraternal or sororal relationships ?

The Catholic Church believes that ordination does not simply give a man permission to perform the functions of a priest, it imparts to him an indelible and permanent spiritual character that makes him a priest. Since Christ and his Apostles chose only men to be priests, only men can validly become priests. The argument continues.....

The spread of Christianity in the first place seems to have led to the gradual dismantling of the belief in the Celtic deities and the high status goddesses. For example, I think that the story of the goddess, *Macha* is an instructive example of the fall from power and grace of Celtic goddesses generally. You could say, it led to the fall of human women as strong, independent beings. This creeping change in culture could be said to only have come into question during modern times. Alas, only in the context of women in the Western world.

This situation demonstrates clearly how the changes that had taken place over the centuries in the Irish stories, due to the change from ancient Celtic religion to Christianity, were now being fixed in law for Earthly women. The changes in Celtic society suggest that by the 19th and 20th centuries, the old stories were interpreted as merely myths, nothing more. Often, Victorian male writers tended to romanticise women as fragile, delicate creatures who needed to be protected and supported by men.

....

When I look back at what I have written, I realise that early Celtic tales tend not to have happy endings ! They are at best bittersweet. Many of them are tragic and speak of the nature of happiness as a brief, passing moment which cannot overcome the inevitable separation of death. I know when my Da and Mam pass on, I will be very sad, grief stricken, but *Aoife* and *Banba,* even *Epona,* will comfort me. I know their souls will be reborn and perhaps I will meet them again, either in an Earthly or Otherworldly form.

However, sadness can also be a source of inner strength. It reminds us to live for the present because death is inevitable. The stories also tell tales of great human qualities like courage, faithfulness and a good soul and spirit. Most of all, they are set in a world of magical forces, where anything is possible and where individuals can shape their own destinies - at least for a while.

(13) Rebirth and Reincarnation

Do not go gentle into that good night,
Old age should burn and rave at close of day;
Rage, rage against the dying of the light.

Though wise men at their end know dark is right,
Because their words had forked no lightning they
Do not go gentle into that good night.

Good men, the last wave by, crying how bright
Their frail deeds might have danced in a green bay,
Rage, rage against the dying of the light.

Wild men who caught and sang the sun in flight,
And learn, too late, they grieved it on its way,
Do not go gentle into that good night.

Grave men, near death, who see with blinding sight
Blind eyes could blaze like meteors and be gay,
Rage, rage against the dying of the light.

And you, my father, there on the sad height,
Curse, bless, me now with your fierce tears, I pray.
Do not go gentle into that good night.
Rage, rage against the dying of the light.

(Dylan Thomas - 1914-1953 – poet & writer)

Date: 2021.

Celtic mythology is imbued with faith in eternal life. While humans, be they heroes and heroines, or livers of a simple life, might die at the end of their physical life, the Celtic gods and goddesses have always assured us that their souls will pass into the undying land of the Otherworld. So in Celtic myth and legend, even tales of death are ultimately a story of rebirth.

Since my first meeting with my sisters from The Otherworld, over half a century ago, I have wondered about being reborn. Will I be reincarnated as a human or another kind of being. Will I take this physical form ? Maybe I will be an animal or a river. I don't want to die, but nevertheless, I am curious about what could come next.

There are different words for rebirth in the English language. Depending on your religion, culture and society, this is a broad umbrella term which can be interpreted in a range and variety of different ways.

I have used a broad brush for my reading over the years which has revealed many aspects of the concept of rebirth. Needless to say, it gets complicated !

In a little Catholic prayer book which Mam gave me on my 5th birthday, there is a prayer to my Guardian Angel. At that time Mam explained that my Guardian Angel was a spiritual being who looked after me. My Angel was sent by God. I have a picture of such a being, which I had on my bedroom wall throughout childhood. When, at the age of 12, I was introduced to *Aoife* and other supernatural beings, I saw them in the same light. My picture shows an Angel represented in human form with wings and a long robe.

My Angel

The Prayer:

Oh Angel of God, who by divine appointment art my Guardian, watch over me in all my ways. Be pleased this day to enlighten, preserve, rule and govern me, whom the goodness of our God has committed to thy charge. Defend me from the powers of darkness.

May the Lord bless us and preserve us from all evils and bring us to life everlasting.
And, may the souls of the faithful departed, through the mercy of God, rest in peace,
Amen

I don't think I understood those words at the age of 5 ! But I was taught to believe whether through the Catholic religion, or the faith in the Otherworld, that I would live on after my earthly death. My Otherworldly guardians may well be considered as the' powers of darkness', by orthodox Christians, even today.

There are suggestions of rebirth and resurrection in most major religions here on Earth. In the Christian church we are taught that we have 3 'places' we might go to after death, namely, Heaven, Hell and Purgatory, also called Limbo. This latter suggests 'waiting' and 'being in between two sets of circumstances'.

According to the Catholic Church, I remember, at school, we were taught 'The parable of the Rich Man and Lazarus' (Luke 16:19-21) Jesus told this story to give all humans an example of what will happen to them after life depending on how they have lived and treated others.

The story goes, there was a rich man who was dressed in purple and fine linen. He feasted sumptuously every day. At the rich man's gate lay a poor man named Lazarus.

He was covered with sores. He was so hungry that he wanted to satisfy his appetite with what fell from the rich man's table. Even the dogs would come and lick his sores. Eventually, the poor man died and was carried away by the angels to be with Abraham. The rich man later died and found himself in Hades, where he was being tormented. He looked up and saw Abraham far away with Lazarus by his side.

He called out, "Father Abraham, have mercy on me, and send Lazarus to dip the tip of his finger in water and cool my tongue, for I am in agony in these flames."

But Abraham said, "Child, remember that during your lifetime you received your good things, and Lazarus in like manner evil things; but now he is comforted here, and you are in agony. Besides all this, between you and us a great chasm has been fixed, so that those who might want to pass from here to you cannot do so, and no one can cross from there to us."

The rich man replied, "Then, father, I beg you to send him to my father's house, for I have five brothers, that he may warn them, so that they will not also come into this place of torment."

Abraham replied, "They have Moses and the prophets; they should listen to them."

The rich man said, "No, father Abraham; but if someone goes to them from the dead, they will repent."

But Abraham said to him, "If they do not listen to Moses and the prophets, neither will they be convinced even if someone rises from the dead."

The parable gives three warnings:

- not to worship material things
- to help those who are in need
- to listen to the prophets

The parable warns us that if these rules are not followed, then an individual will end up in Hell. I found this very scary when I heard it at around the age of 8. Our priest, Father Donnelly, in a scary, booming voice, implied that even our childish 'sins' could condemn us to eternity in Hell. We could only prevent this by being good and saying our prayers !

Later, when I asked my sister, *Aoife* about these teachings, she would only smile and say, "wait, listen and watch and you will learn. Then you can decide for yourself."

This did scare me because I wasn't confident that I could make the right choices. Sometimes the line between 'good' and 'bad' is not straight. The road ahead may be blurred and misty.

What else was I taught as a Catholic girl ?

What is Heaven ?

Heaven was described to us children as 'eternity in the presence of God'. It's a state of being, rather than a physical place. A pretty difficult concept to imagine as a child. Once I met my Otherworldly sisters and increasingly saw examples of what might be in store, I became more settled, albeit still curious and excited.

Heaven is the ultimate aim for all Catholics, so that their souls can be reunited with God and his Son.

In the gospels of the Bible, Christ often describes and teaches about Heaven using parables, For example,

"In my Father's house there are many dwelling places. If it were not so, would I have told you that I go to prepare a place for you? And if I go and prepare a place for you, I will come again and will take you to myself, so that where I am, there you may be also. And you know the way to the place where I am going. " (from the Bible's New Testament, John 14:1-4)

What is Hell ?

Since God has given human beings free will, there must be an opportunity for people to reject God. This is the basis of the idea of Hell. Hell has traditionally been depicted as a place of eternal fire that symbolises pain and suffering. This is seen as the result of the refusal to accept the happiness that God wants people to share with him. Hell is the opposite of Heaven. It means spending eternity in the absence of God.

The Catholic Church also teaches that after death there is a state of Purgatory. (Maybe not for Saints ?) This is a place where people who have sinned are purified in a 'cleansing fire', after which they are accepted into Heaven. Fire is often referred to as cleansing.

Purgatory is a condition, a process, or place of purification or temporary punishment in which, according to medieval Christian and Roman Catholic belief, the souls of those who die in a state of grace are prepared for heaven.

From The Catechism of the Catholic Church which is used to teach children and adults about life after death:

"All who die in God's grace and friendship, but still imperfectly purified, are indeed assured of their eternal salvation: but after death they undergo purification, so as to achieve the holiness necessary to enter the joy of Heaven."

Rebirth in Buddhism refers to the teaching that the actions of a person lead to a new existence after death, in an endless cycle called *saṃsāra*. This cycle is considered to be *dukkha*. Not something heavenly, but rather unsatisfactory and painful. The cycle stops only if *moksha* (liberation) is achieved. How can that be achieved ? Apparently, through insight and the extinguishing of craving. It's like the Lazarus story. In modern terms, not being materialistic or greedy in terms of the acquisition of money, property or 'things'. Gaining insight seems to me to be more in tune with learning gained over time. The latter is interesting in the context of our increasingly materialistic world here on this planet and humans' loss of being at one with nature.

Rebirth is one of the basic doctrines of Buddhism. There's also *karma, Nirvana* and *Moksha*. The rebirth doctrine is sometimes referred by Buddists as *reincarnation* or *transmigration*. The belief is that rebirth doesn't necessarily take place as another human being, but can also lead to an existence in one of the six realms of existence, which also include heaven , the animal realm, the ghost realm and hell.

Rebirth, determined by *karma*, would mean being reborn into a good realm, favoured by *kushala* (meaning good or skilful karma). Rebirth into the evil realms is a consequence of *akushala* , what we call 'bad karma'. *Nirvana* is the ultimate goal of Buddhist teaching and traditional practice. It focuses on gaining merit and transfer of merit. Through such merit, a person gains rebirth in the good realms and avoids rebirth in the evil realms !

Some Buddhist traditions assert that *vijñana* (consciousness), is constantly changing. Nevertheless, it exists as a continuum or stream called *Santana*. It is this condition which undergoes rebirth. The stream of consciousness has been used by writers as a narrative device that attempts to give the written equivalent of the character's thought processes. Quite a task as I well know ! It has been used since the 19th century by a range of well-known novelists. There are variations on these ideas across Buddist society.

Reincarnation is in fact, central to all main Indian religions and most varieties of Paganism as well. Some don't call it reincarnation. They believe in an 'afterlife'. Indigenous peoples of America and Australia, think of an afterlife as a spirit world. This seems more like the Celtic view.

A belief in rebirth was held by Greek historical figures, such as Pythagoras, Socrates, and Plato and by the Romans. As an example, I know that In his work, 'The Republic', Plato makes Socrates tell the tale of how *Er*, the son of *Armenius*, miraculously returned to life on the twelfth day (notice the multiple of 3) after death and told of the secrets of the Otherworld.

I find it interesting now, that in this modern age, many Europeans and Americans have developed an interest in rebirth / reincarnation. There are numerous contemporary accounts in fiction and non-fiction formats. Film and computer games are other genres which have used the idea of rebirth or reincarnation as a key to mind-changing self-discovery.

It's difficult, when I speak to those I don't know well, to put over my views. Often people will ask "Is there any solid evidence for what you claim ?" "Where are your sources ?" I was asked this when hinting that I was thinking about publishing my journal. As one friend asked, "Is reincarnation or rebirth really possible from a scientific, or even rational, point of view?"

I have pointed out that I'm not writing an academic thesis. I am not carrying out any experiments. There are no concrete measurements ! Then the response is, "So it's fiction then ?"

Well, it's real for me and others I know. How much is from my imagination and how much is what some might call 'physical' reality, is for others to decide. I am comfortable in my own skin. That's what matters to me.

---

(14) Chivalry - The Quest For Honour

Date: It's Easter 1968 and, yippee, it's the school holidays !

Although I often think that our parish priest, Father Donnelly is a miserable old man. He's even older than my Mam and Da ! Nevertheless, he came into school on the last day of term and told us the story of Jesus' crucifixion. I've heard it many times, but this time, he went into more detail and treated us more like adults than children for a change.

The more I think about Jesus, the more I think he must have been the son of God, or at least a god. Father Donnelly began by asking a question. "Why was Jesus crucified ?" I waited for the answer with baited breath.

This is what we found out about why Jesus died according to the Scriptures:

- To carry our sins and take the punishment as representative of mankind.
- To overcome the evil in our hearts, by showing us a better way.
- To overcome death and give us assurance of the resurrection and eternal life through his own resurrection.
- To carry our shame in our stead.
- To show how much He loves us.
- To show how much God hates sin.
- To remove any legal right that Satan might have on earth and on us.

The leaders and, the chief priests of his day decided that Jesus had to die for a number of reasons…

He obviously couldn't be a main religious leader because he came from a small village called Nazareth, situated in Galilee. They thought he was some kind of 'local yokel', telling lies and misleading the common people.

He had a group of followers, called disciples. They, together with many ordinary people believed Jesus to be the promised Messiah.

However, the traditional leaders believed he was threatening the Jewish leadership by preaching different ideas. He didn't act like they expected a King or Messiah to act.

Jesus claimed to be the Son of God and one with God. To the orthodox view, this was blasphemy. The more popular Jesus became among the common people, there was a very real danger that the Romans might react violently against the whole of the Jewish people, destroying the temples and their status as leaders in Jerusalem. Pontius Pilate, who was the Roman governor of the area called Judaea , was the one who presided at the trial of Jesus and gave the order for his crucifixion.

Pontius Pilate had decided that Jesus had to die for totally different reasons. He actually had conversations with Jesus and decided that he was not involved in any plans for violent rebellion, as claimed by the Jewish leaders.

Pontius Pilate knew that by crucifying the man he called "King of the Jews", he was mocking the whole Jewish people. Crucifixion was a shameful death. He knew that if he let Jesus go, against the wishes of the Jewish leadership, he could then be held responsible for any future rebellion, if Jesus claimed he was the Messiah.

Pilate didn't really know what to make of Jesus' silence when he was being accused. While he didn't find any evidence against Jesus, he was surprised that Jesus didn't defend himself against those claims. It worried him.

While the disciples plainly did not expect Jesus to be crucified if he was the Messiah King, as stated in the gospels, Jesus explained to them that this was according to what had been pre-ordained .This made me think of the idea of what had been said to be pre-destined by the ancient Celtic gods and goddesses. *Aoife* has told me that they don't interfere with the future. She doesn't elaborate. Has it already been decided ? I think there's room for change, but I'm not sure.

When Father Donnelly asked if we had any questions, I thought I'd better not ask such a question in case he would think me an atheist !! But, I know that atheists don't believe in any deities, so that's certainly not me !

I still haven't said anything directly to Mam and Da about my visits from *Aoife* or time spent with *Banba*. I believe it's unsaid because it's pre-destined and doesn't need to be discussed. They believe this, but they don't know my future and neither do I.

After the first visit from *Aoife*, I found one of Da's books which tells the story of her falling out with her sister *Scáthach*. This is a story which stretches back into the mists of time.

These stories have been passed from generation to generation. In one of Da's books, it says the stories were first passed on by Minstrels, employed as travelling entertainers and later, some as a castle or court musician or medieval Bard. They performed songs which told stories of distant times and places and Earthly and Otherworldly events which had taken place. Although Minstrels did create their own tales, often they would memorise and embellish the works of others. In this way many of the same stories were repeated, but different versions would emerge over time. A minstrel was a servant first. The name 'minstrel' means a 'little servant'.

A Minstrel

As well as Minstrels there were Troubadours (trouvère). They were poets and musicians. They were often of knightly rank, so had higher status than a Minstrel. They were commonplace from the 11th to the 13th century. They were mainly found in the South of France and the North of Italy. They sang about courtly love, as well as popular folk songs.

Troubadours (trouvère)

I know from other stories that are still passed around, that chivalry was very important to warriors. They were like knights led by chieftains, who ruled the land, like kings. The warriors were very proud of their heritage and their civilisation. No wonder, *Aoife* was so devastated by the trickery of *Cuchullain.*

Da has explained to me another reason why we know so much about these ancient deeds. It's because all of the warrior groups had their own '*Seanachie'*. This was an important person who was responsible for telling the tales of all the brave deeds in battle. *Cuchullain* was one of the most famous characters. There are hundreds of stories about his heroic deeds which, incredibly, have lasted until now. Da says we could argue about whether they were real or imaginary tales, but nobody really knows the answer. I have always liked to think they are real deeds carried out by beings who had magical powers. That seemed more exciting.

Now I have met *Aoife* and *Banba* and heard their tales, I realise that stories do get changed over the centuries. These tales are very much from an oral tradition, so different versions now exist in writing.

I want to find out more about *Cúchulainn,* so Da borrowed a book from the university library. This explains that he was an Irish, mythological demi-god who appears in the stories of the 'Ulster Cycle', as well as in Scottish and Manx mythology.

The 'Ulster Cycle' (*an Rúraíocht*) was one of the four great cycles of Irish mythology. It's a collection of medieval Irish heroic legends and sagas. Traditional heroes were from Ulster *(Ulaid)*. The stories are set in the 1st century BC, although they may date from an even earlier time. I know now that time, as we know it, is different from time as known by beings from the Otherworld.

Much later in our history, between the 8th and 11th centuries AD, the stories were recorded in written documents. They have been preserved in the 12th-century manuscripts known as 'The Book of the Dun Cow'. They may have been changed, exaggerated and developed over time and gradually become presented as myths and legends involving supernatural, otherworldly life forms rather than stories from history.

I have learnt that *Cuchullain* was the nephew and foster son of *King Conor* of *Emania*. This is a story I read about him. When *Cuchullain* was young, he arrived at the Court one day. A group of boys of his own age were playing a game called *Camán* (hurling). He had brought with him an impressive red, bronze hurley (a stick used for playing hurling). He played brilliantly, far better than the others. The people of the Court were impressed. They believed that this was a sign that he would have a great future. In addition, the warriors acknowledged him as a blood relative of the King.

Some time later, he was sent to see the Druids, priests and priestesses, in 'The Hall of Heroes.' He proudly announced to them:

*"I care not whether I die tomorrow or next year,
if only my deeds live after me".*

After his son had been born and he had left his family, *Cuchulainn* achieved great deeds as a warrior. One of his greatest deeds was said to be when, all alone, he held back the armed forces of Connaught.

The next part of the story really struck a chord with me, bearing in mind what I know happened later. Unfortunately, he had to fight a friend, *Ferdiad*, who was now the champion and chief of the Connaught Knights of the Sword. The pair had been trained together as young men in *Alba* (Scotland) by none other than the great warrior *Scáthach* !

Cuchullain tried to negotiate a deal with his friend, but *Ferdiad* refused.

Cuchullain reminded him by saying, "We were heart companions, We were companions in the woods, We were fellows of the same bed, where we used to sleep the balmy sleep. After mortal battles abroad, In countries many and far distant, together we used to practice, and go through each forest, learning with *Scáthach*".

Ferdiad would not change his mind. So they fought for four days and eventually, as they both were weakening, *Cuchullain* killed *Ferdiad*. He was very sad and sorry. How ironic that he went on to kill his son.

Frustratingly, I found there is not much written information about *Scathach*. She remains a shadowy figure. She is certainly a strong and powerful independent goddess and respected and loved by the supernatural warriors who train with her. No doubt, her amazing skills are the result of magic. She is a character from the Otherworld, yet is sometimes presented as an Earthly woman. Maybe a mixture of both ? *Aoife* too ? I'd love to know. I know that Earthly people can be reborn after death, so is it the same for those of the Otherworld ? Possibly not, because they already have the ability to shape-shift and seemingly live for ever; at least in the confines of our perception of time. Maybe I will find out in the future.

Eventually, *Cuchulainn* himself died on the battlefield. His fellow warriors propped his body up against a large rock. They put a spear in his hand and a 'buckler' (a small round shield) on his arm. They thought he still looked like a fierce warrior and would still be able to strike fear into his enemies.

After *Aoife* had lost both *Cuchulainn* and *Connla*, she later was known to be one of the wives of King *Lir* in the story, '*Oidheadh chloinne Lir*', (Fate of the Children of *Lir*). This is another Irish myth. It has worried me since I read it. Was this the being I met ? Or another *Aoife* ? Maybe, losing both her lover and her son made her disillusioned and bitter ? How will that affect me ?

I have always loved swans and stories about them. Da read me this poem by his favourite poet, William Butler Yeats. It's a beautiful poem. Da has explained that the swans in the poem are symbols. They symbolise beauty, grace and energy, The poem gives them a mythical status. They are portrayed as divine creatures. As such, they remain unchanged despite everything that has changed in the life of the man writing the story of the poem . The swans are unmoved by time and even immune to pain and tiredness.

The Wild Swans at Coole

The trees are in their autumn beauty,
The woodland paths are dry,
Under the October twilight the water
Mirrors a still sky;
Upon the brimming water among the stones
Are nine-and-fifty swans.

The nineteenth autumn has come upon me
Since I first made my count;
I saw, before I had well finished,
All suddenly mount
And scatter wheeling in great broken rings
Upon their clamorous wings.

I have looked upon those brilliant creatures,
And now my heart is sore.
All's changed since I, hearing at twilight,
The first time on this shore,
The bell-beat of their wings above my head,
Trod with a lighter tread.

Unwearied still, lover by lover,
They paddle in the cold
Companionable streams or climb the air;
Their hearts have not grown old;
Passion or conquest, wander where they will,
Attend upon them still.

But now they drift on the still water,
Mysterious, beautiful;
Among what rushes will they build,
By what lake's edge or pool
Delight men's eyes when I awake some day
To find they have flown away?

(W.B. Yeats – 1865 – 1939 - Irish poet, dramatist, prose writer)

Many years ago in ancient Ireland, lived a King and ruler of the sea called *Lir*. He had a beautiful wife, called *Eva*. They had 4 children. The eldest son was *Aodh*, then a daughter called *Fionnula*, and the youngest, twin boys, *Fiachra* and *Conn*.

When the children were very young, their mother *Eva* sadly died. King *Lir* and his children were very miserable. The King decided that the best thing would be to find a new wife and mother for his children. So, he married *Eva*'s sister *Aoife*. She was very beautiful and possessed magical powers. Judging from what I already know about *Aoife*, I think this must have been during another time in the Otherworld. I will ask her. I am a bit puzzled, though. She told me that she was known as a protector of children and the vulnerable, but this story demonstrates another side to her.

Aoife loved King *Lir* and the children at first. Unfortunately, soon she became very jealous of all the time that the King spent with his children. She wanted to have all his attention for herself.

One hot, sunny day, she took the children for a swim in the lake. The children were thrilled and soon jumped into the water. When they got there and children took to the water, *Aoife* had an idea. She didn't want to harm them, so used her powers to cast a spell over them. While they swam happily in the water, she turned them all into beautiful swans.

However, she did not want them to come back and haunt her. She cast another spell. They would live as swans for 900 years, spending 300 years on each of 3 lakes: Lake Derravaragh, the Straits of Moyle, and the Isle of Inish Glora. The spell would only be broken if and when the children heard the ringing of a bell, announcing the arrival of St. Patrick in Ireland.

Aoife's spell had changed the children's form, but had not taken away their voices. King *Lir*, who had been searching for his children, came down to the lake. Four elegant swans were swimming and singing beautiful songs. Through such a song, they were able to tell their father what had happened to them. The King was very angry. He banished *Aoife* into the mist.

Some say *Aoife* was turned into a crane-like bird and condemned to spend eternity in the skies. Cranes are now regarded as good luck omens because they depart the countryside in times of war. If they fly over, that suggests that peace will prevail. The story also said that she took the form of a crane because she was sad about what she had done.

Knowing she had done wrong, she accepted her fate. I like to think that because this embodiment of *Aoife* had learned her lesson, she remains flying in the sky for eternity, bringing peace, beauty and radiance to the children of the world.

I have also discovered that the relationship between women and birds is a constant theme in folklore and myth all over the world. For example, the 'battle-crow' is also a title given to a number of ancient female warriors.

The story continues and tells us that although he was saddened by his children's fate, King *Lir* remained a good father and he spent his days resting by the lake, listening to their heavenly singing.

The children's first 300 years on Lake Derravaragh were filled with joy, but at end of this first part of their spell, they had to say goodbye to their father forever. They travelled across to Straits of Moyle. This was a sorry time for them. They spent the next 300 years enduring fierce storms. They spent long periods of time separated from each other. Nevertheless, they clung together. Eventually, they travelled, together to complete the final stage of the spell. They found some peace on a small saltwater lake on Isle of *Inish Glora*.

By this time King *Lir* had aged and died. His once magnificent palace was no more than a ruin. One day, the swans heard the distant ringing of a bell. It was one of the first Christian bells in all of Ireland. They felt drawn by the sound and followed it. Remembering the original spell, they knew the end of their shape-shifting was near. They followed the ringing of the bells to the house of a holy man called *Caomhog*, who cared for them.

One day though, disaster struck again. A man came to the house. He was a soldier, dressed in armour.

" I am the King of Connacht," he announced. "I have come for the magical, mystical swans with the beautiful singing voices. Give them to me or I shall tear down this house."

He leaned over and touched the swans. As he did so, the bell tolled again. A thick mist appeared. It enveloped the swans and swirled around them. They were changed back into the children they had been 900 years before.

The King of Connacht was terrified by this magic. He fled immediately.
Back in their natural state, the human children began to age rapidly. *Caomhog* knew that they soon would die. As a new Christian, he hurriedly christened them before their human bodies passed away. In this way, he knew that their legend and their names would live on forever. We still know of them today as the 'Children of Lir'.

I like to think that maybe the mist was *Aoife* undoing her spell and allowing the children to pass on to the next world as they would have done naturally. If I feel brave enough, I'll ask her about it when I see her.

King Lir with his children who were turned into swans.

I wondered how Tchaikovsky got the idea for the ballet 'Swan Lake', as he was Russian and wouldn't have heard an Irish folk story. Da explained that there are many stories around the world where the idea of a human being changed into a swan was central to the plot.

Rudolf Nureyev and Margot Fonteyn

Knowing the story, I was keen to see Swan Lake performed as a ballet. In 1964, the wonderful dancers, Rudolf Nureyev and Margot Fonteyn, performed the ballet in London. As a special treat for my 11th birthday, I went to see it with my Mam, Da and my Aunt Brigid, who has a flat in London and a holiday cottage in Norfolk. She is a lecturer and researcher at Cambridge University. We were able to stay with her in London.

Swan Lake is a love story that mixes magic, tragedy and romance based on good and evil characters. The main characters are Prince Siegfried and a lovely swan princess called Odette. A sorcerer casts a spell and changes Odette into a swan. She is to be found swimming on a lake of tears during the day. At night, she returns to her human form as a beautiful princess.

The couple meet and fall in love. As a folk or fairy tale, things are made difficult for them by the sorcerer. He would like his daughter Odile to marry Prince Siegfried. Through his magic tricks, he causes much confusion. Eventually, there is a happy ending. Prince Siegfried and Odette get back together forever. The story begins with Prince Siegfried arriving at his 21st birthday party which is held in the palace courtyard. He finds all the royal families and local people dancing and celebrating. Because he is so handsome, all the girls are keen to get his attention.

During the elaborate celebration, the Prince's mother gives him a crossbow. She tells him that he is now an adult. He must get married as soon as possible. The young Prince is worried about this and all the responsibilities it will bring. He decides to take his crossbow and he goes off to the woods to hunt with his friends.

Prince Siegfried runs faster than the others and finds himself alone in a quiet and peaceful spot by an enchanted lake. Here, the swans gently glide across its surface. While he watches, he sees a swan who is the most lovely of them all. She has a crown on her head.

His friends soon catch him up, but he orders them to go away so that he can be alone. Dusk falls.

I imagine this time as magical. Dusk brings moonlight. The Prince reflects on the day of his birthday. I see him waiting quietly until the day is renewed by the light of the dawn sun. I like dusk. It's when the birds sing goodnight. They settle and putting their feathered heads under their wings, they sleep. The stars appear and send dreams to the birds. The colours of the sky deepen and quiet descends.

The dawn comes and the sun begins to rise. The swan wearing the crown turns into the most beautiful young woman the Prince has ever seen. Her name is Odette, the Swan Queen.
Odette tells him about the evil sorcerer. He is Von Rothbart, who has disguised himself as Prince Siegfried's mentor. It was Von Rothbart who turned her and the other girls into swans. She explains that the lake of tears was created from the tears of their parents' weeping. She confides in him that the only way the spell can be broken is if a man, who is pure in heart, pledges his love to her.

The prince is captivated. He is about to declare his love for her, when they are quickly interrupted by the evil sorcerer. He takes Odette away from Prince Siegfried's embrace. He then commands all of the swan maidens to dance upon the lake and its shore so that the Prince cannot chase them. Poor Prince Siegfried is left all alone on the shore of Swan Lake. The next day there is a formal birthday celebration in the Royal Hall. Prince Siegfried is presented with many princesses who might make suitable wives for him. Unfortunately for them, Prince Seigfried cannot stop thinking about Odette.

His mother insists he must choose a bride, but he doesn't want to. However, he agrees to dance with the princesses to keep his mother happy.

While the prince dances, trumpets announce the arrival of Von Rothbart. He brings his daughter, Odile with him. Unbeknown to anyone else, he has cast a spell to make her look just like Odette. The prince is once more captivated by her beauty and he dances with the imposter.

Unbeknown to Prince Siegfried, the real Odette is watching him from a window. She is horrified when she hears the Prince declare his love for Odile. He proposes marriage to her, thinking, of course, that she is Odette.

Odette is devastated. She runs off into the night. Suddenly, Prince Siegfried sees her running away and realises his mistake. Von Rothbart witnesses this and quickly reveals to the prince the true appearance of his daughter Odile. Prince Siegfried is horrified. He rushes away from the party and chases after Odette.

Odette runs to the lake and joins the other girls. She tells them what she thinks has happened. Prince Siegfried finds them all gathered together at the shore consoling Odette. He explains to Odette the trickery of Von Rothbart. She immediately forgives him.

The drama is not over. Von Rothbart and Odile appear. This time the Prince and the girls see both of them in their evil, inhuman forms. They look like ugly birds. The heads are black and the beak is long. When the beak is opened, it reveals silver teeth, each a thin, serrated blade which looks as sharp as a sword's edge.

Von Rothbart tells the prince that he must marry his daughter. There is a fight. Prince Siegfried finally tells Von Rothbart that he would rather die with Odette than marry Odile. He takes Odette's hand and together they jump into the lake.

The spell is broken. The other girls all turn back into humans. They quickly drive Von Rothbart and Odile into the water where, like the lovers, they drown. The girls watch as the spirits of Prince Siegfried and Odette ascend into the heavens above Swan Lake. I loved watching the ballet because Margot Fonteyn danced so beautifully as Odette. She gracefully flowed across the stage just like an elegant swan moving.

When she is returned to her human form, she is less confident and comfortable. As a swan, she is serene, though she often feels lonely at night. Prince Siegfried has his life limited by his royal responsibilities. He is aware that his future has been decided already. He finally rebels follows his heart for love.

It's a true fairy tale in that sense. It's the fight between good and evil. The fact that one ballerina plays two opposites emphasises the conflict. Outwardly, the two girls are identical, but inside their souls, one is good and the other is bad. The wicked Von Rothbart and his daughter, Odile keep the tension going. Good does win in the end, although all the characters die. I think, perhaps, it's a bit like soldiers dying in a battle for the greater good.

(15) We Are Stardust

Well, I came upon a child of God
He was walking along the road
And I asked him, "Tell me, where are you going?"
And this he told me
Said, "I'm going down to Yasgur's Farm
Gonna join in a rock 'n' roll band
Got to get back to the land
Set my soul free"

We are stardust, we are golden
We are billion-year-old carbon
And we've got to get ourselves
Back to the garden
Well, then can I walk beside you?
I have come to lose the smog

And I feel myself a cog
In somethin' turning
And maybe it's the time of year
Yes, and maybe it's the time of man
And I don't know who I am
But life is for learning

We are stardust, we are golden
We are billion-year-old carbon
And we got to get ourselves
Back to the garden
We are stardust, we are golden
We are billion-year-old carbon
And we got to get ourselves
Back to the garden
By the time we got to Woodstock
We were half a million strong
And everywhere was a song
And a celebration
And I dreamed I saw the bomber jet planes
Riding shotgun in the sky
Turning into butterflies
Above our nation
We are stardust, we are golden
We are caught in the devil's bargain
And we've got to get ourselves
Back to the garden.

(song - Crosby, Stills & Nash, 1970)

Date:2021

Imagine though, for a moment, approaching the 'issue' (not a 'problem', as some suggest) of where we come from and what we are made of. I might say 'Stardust' – millions and billions of tiny pieces which float in The Ether and are gathered up to make a heterogeneity - the quality or state of being , diverse in character or content.

From the point of view of science, a parallel which might be applicable could be 'quantum mechanics'.

What's that when it's at home ?' I have been asked. As it's a discipline which I readily admit I understand practically nothing about, you might ask why I am trying to do such an exercise. Jumping in at the deep end, I suppose. I've learned to do that. Now that I'm old, maybe you might think I'm just a potty old bat. Bear with me.

A dictionary definition is: 'Quantum mechanics is a fundamental theory in physics that provides a description of the physical properties of nature at the scale of atoms and subatomic particles.'

It's fascinating to think that everything both in our Earthly world and elsewhere in the universe: the Otherworld, consists of what scientists call 'quantum particles'. These particles, or tiny pieces, can exist in one place or another, even at the same time. The official definition explains that all the possibilities described by quantum theory, occur simultaneously in what is referred to as a "multiverse". I like this word.

Physical places and periods of time are concepts that we use to bring us to the 'quantum level'. I know, from my interaction with supernatural beings, that such concepts don't exist at the quantum level. Even if they did, they would be created only as we humans on Earth apply them. Scientists use measurements, as we understand them, to give these complex 'things' some meaning to humans, but not necessarily to other beings.

For instance, we speak of dimensions. That can mean something measurable, like, let's say, length. Dimension can also be an aspect of a situation. For example, a cultural dimension.

A third definition is some kind of form or shape which conforms to particular measurements. I can only describe my Otherworldly contacts in terms of things human. For instance, *Aoife* appears to be about the same height as me, although she is not solid flesh. She exudes brightness, radiance with her golden hair and blue eyes. She is a protector of children. But, she is more than that. She exists across millennia, even eons, of time ! Possibly eternity.

Scientists also refer to something called 'string theory'. It's apparently, a branch of theoretical physics. It's not tying yourself up in knots ! A 'string' is an object with a one-dimensional spatial extent, whereas an elementary particle is zero-dimensional, like a point. That is hard to grasp - for me at least. What is one dimensional, as opposed to zero dimensional ? To me, if something has no dimensions, then it is nothing. It can't exist.

That's not the case though. Something one-dimensional is actually there. Of course it's very, very, small in human terms. It is no larger than the 'Planck' length. That's according to one of Da's books. A Planck length is the smallest distance or size about which anything can be known. The word came from a scientist called Max Planck, at the end of the 19[Th] century.

Mr Planck proposed a universal set of units for length, time, mass, temperature and other physical qualities. He was trying to come up with a way to define units that depended only on constants of the Universe. This idea from a scientist is, I think, similar to the medieval idea of something called 'The Ether'. I think of the word as existing in the Otherworld. Something not solid, like a mystical mist. Or, more down to earth, when I can't find something, I say it must have disappeared into the Ether !

In medieval times, magicians believed that 'The Ether' was something that could be transformed into matter, energy or 'essence', through the use of spells. Something I think of being connected to fairies or witches. The spells were made so as to detect disturbances in the flow of The Ether.

Centuries later, scientists still talk of disturbances in The Ether. Gravitational effects by which quantum particles are said to make their presence known. If The Ether can be transformed into either matter and energy, then magicians were there before Einstein. In one book I read, it suggested that $E=m2$ can be thought of as originating in a supernatural, magic spell ! Sorry Albert !

Whether in human science, or in its Otherworld equivalent, both quantum particles and The Ether can be thought of as something that is everywhere. Ultimately, it's everything. All beings, and everything around us, consist entirely in, and of, it. This includes our bodies and our minds. We consist of one-dimensional 'bits' of the cosmos. All and each of us, in our miniscule way, have organised ourselves, both personally and collectively, in such a way as to make sense of what has been called 'chaos'. We might seem zero-dimensional from a distance, but upon closer inspection we may be more interesting, even have a lot to offer. For instance, friendship with the others who share The Ether. The Otherworldly. The Aliens….

All life is born and becomes beings of one sort or another. Our consciousness is the gravitation which sets us on our planet. We came from a swirling, whirling nothing and one day we may return to that. In between, or instead, we live, are reborn and so on in a never-ending cycle. We have been and will be reincarnated as part of the huge range and variety of everything there is. We will be males, females, animals, trees, rivers, suns, moons or stars. Our individual identities are assembled from these particles of dust, or The Ether. Name it as you see fit.

---

(10) Aoife, Otherworldly Warrior Queen

Scáthach- sister of Aoife

I left out a few facts when I spoke to my latest young Earthly sister. My Otherworld sister, Scáthach, is no longer my sister or my soul-mate. We are both skilled warriors, but now, we are war.

All was well, until Cuchullain came to train with Scáthach. She fell in love with him. He was the most important person in her life. She became obsessed. She even accused me of trying to take him away from her, so that I might have him for myself.

During his training in arms under Scáthach, a battle between she and I broke out. Scáthach, was worried about Cuchullain's safety. After all, he was now her champion. So, she gave him a sleeping potion to keep him out of the battle. Unluckily for her, I cast a spell to reverse the effects of the potion. I couldn't stop him falling asleep, but due to my magic, it only knocked him out for about an hour. Then, he came to join the fight. To avoid him being injured, as well as not upsetting my sister, I challenged Scáthach to single combat. Instead, Cuchullain intervened and insisted on engaging in combat with me on Scáthach's behalf. I had no choice but to begin to fight.

Soon, I shattered Cuchullain's sword. He knew he was finished. Instead of accepting his defeat like a man, he played a cruel trick on me. He knew that what I love most in a battle is my chariot and horses. At that moment, he cried out to me that my chariot and horses had fallen over a cliff. When I turned to look, in that fleeting speck of time, he overpowered me. To my indignation, he threw me over his shoulder and carried me back to where Scáthach's troops were waiting. He held his sword at my throat. I prepared to die. He stopped as Scáthach approached. He knew that despite our sisterly differences, Scáthach would not want him to kill me on her behalf. It would undermine her authority as a chivalrous warrior trainer. He decided not to kill me on two conditions. The first was that I ceased hostilities with Scáthach which I was prepared to do. Then, to my surprise, he told me it was I that he loved and not my sister. I must admit I had been attracted to him. Jealousy was part of the reason for the hostilities between myself and Scáthach.

Scáthach looked on in fury as I gave in to his demands.

The Warrior *Cuchullain*

Cuchullain and I became lovers and soon, I bore him a son. As god and goddess, of course, we knew before he was born that the baby would be a boy.

Shortly after our son was born, I was surprised and angry when Cuchullain told me he had to leave. He did not tell me why he was deserting us. He swore he would return, but he could not say when in Earth years. I was angry and upset. I had trusted him. Before he left, he gave me a gold ring to give to our child. He said that, through his magic, by the time the boy reached just 7 years old, he would be a proficient warrior.

"You will train him," he advised, "so that we shall both be proud of him. When he reaches the age of seven, I will send him a message and he will have to set off and find me. However, on his travels he must not let anyone know his true identity."

I promised I would do this. I believed that Cuchullain would greet his son and welcome him. It was some compensation for losing my lover.

*Seven years later, our son, who we had called
Connla, received a message from his father in a dream.
Connla learnt that his father, Cuchullain, had returned to Earth
and was in Ireland. I sent Connla to find his father as
instructed. Despite his age, I had taught Connla to be a good
warrior. I cannot tell you how it broke my heart to lose my son,
but I knew in my heart he would return. He would find his
father and all would be well. Perhaps we three might be
together again.*

*Through our extrasensory perception, Connla kept me
informed of his progress. He had, as promised, kept his
identity secret.*

*One day, I discovered that Cuchullain had heard of a boy who
had great warrior skills. At last father and son would meet.
However, to my horror, I found that Cuchullain had decided
that the boy was a threat to him. As instructed, Connla would
not identify himself. He did not know this being who
threatened him was his own father.*

*Because of his wariness and distrust of the young warrior,
Cuchullain challenged him to fight a duel. He killed him. As my
darling boy lay dying, too late, Cuchullain recognised the gold
ring he had given our child and realised that he had killed his
only son.*

Connla is fatally wounded

I should have warned Connla to be wary, but Cuchullain's power was too strong. He held back my warnings. I conjured up the scene and watched Cuchullain's pain emerge. I was bereft, yet hatred for Cuchullain coursed through my soul.

Cuchullain staggered away from the scene. Under his boots the golden leaves were as noisy as the static I had sent to him, now buzzing unbearably in his head. With one hand he leant against an ancient oak, his fingertips gripping into the crevices that ran through the bark. His eyes came to rest on the pattern there, chaotic, age-hardened cracks jumping out at him. Nothing was making sense anymore, not even trees. His life had lost direction and meaning. Despite his godly powers, all his plans had been for Connla and their life together, their future. Now, he was gone and at his own hand. There seemed no reason for his world to exist anymore. Why was it all still here? Solid and unchanged ? He willed the natural world to dissolve around him, just to melt away. He closed his eyes, yet still he could still feel the rough bark. He pressed his hands hard into it until he drew blood.

I, Aoife, sent a chill, freezing wind to pierce his heart and magnify the howling pain that I could feel had torn through his body. Its vocal expression poisoned the air. I watched with a mixture of sorrow and revenge as he felt his insides become icy. He is a villain and a coward.

(17) Meeting Epona

Date 1969

Today, I'm going for a ride on my own with Epona. I want to canter bareback. Mam is confident that I'm ready. We have spent plenty of time lunging her. It's essential to be able to keep your balance when travelling in a relatively tight circle. On the lunge it's essential to concentrate on maintaining your seat.

Mam always emphasises this. "Keep your legs long and heels down," she says. "Think of letting your weight sink through your natural seat cushions and down through your legs. Keep your seat springy. Stay relaxed and flexible and do not forget to breathe. Remember, holding your breath keeps your weight high and will not be comfortable for you or Epona."

I also know that when riding bareback, if I did start to lose my balance, I mustn't clench with my legs. Otherwise, Epona might take this as a cue to go faster. She's very good at sensing my situation. If I hold a handful of her mane to steady myself, she knows why I'm doing it. Mam says many people have a tendency to lean back and let their legs push forward, or they hunch forward and bring their heels up.

"Either of these will lessen your overall security and skill," she warns.

Mam told me before I left, " just remember, leaning back too far means if Epona moves suddenly, you might get left behind !!"

Today it's time for a longer ride. So, I'm heading out alone. Epona and I moving as one. We are going to head out towards the track that encircles the grounds of Blarney Castle. I know that if the worst came to the worst, and I did slip off, or had to dismount for some reason, I might have to make creative use of rocks, logs, or fences !

I'm also aware that going up steep inclines can be a challenge without a saddle.

Mam's advice is "lean forward to get your weight off the horse's back and use handfuls of mane to prevent you sliding backward. Whatever you do, do not use the reins for balance. That will confuse and could hurt her."

I take all this in, but I'm impatient to go, as is Epona. Mam waves as I leave the paddock. We're off !

Epona's mane sparkles in the sunlight which has followed a shower of rain. She seems to be sweeping through the air. I can feel her rising upward. Once on the track, Epona and I sense a new freedom. She is soon in full flight. As I hold her mane, her body returns to the solidity of the earth, hooves lightly landing on the quenched grassland. As she and I become one, each second of time expands. It's like riding in slow motion. Her mane, still bright, twists in front of my eyes and takes the shape of a tree trunk. The wispy ends become branches reaching outward. We race ahead, a vision of girl and steed riding in perfect harmony.

I am a Celtic female warrior, riding my war horse. In each noble breath upon the field where goodness makes its stand against evil, the spirit of *Epona* towers above mortal men. I am a goddess. Our souls are pure. The war horse and the warrior standing their ground as strongly as any mighty oak ever could. Together we have bravery enough to fill the verses of many a bard's ballad for centuries, to come.

The dream fades and Epona slows. We have stopped by a large oak tree, its lower branches stretching out like arms. A perfect place to dismount. Once again we are on the edge of the forest, known in the Otherworld as The Woodland. I'd like to hug the tree, but it's so wide my arms would barely stretch halfway. Epona waits patiently while I dismount. I slip her reins round the branch.

I have learned from *Banba* that there is a wisdom in the oldest of trees that can be whispered to those pure in heart. The forest and every tree in it, has its own unique soul, just as we Earthly beings have in our world. When I was younger, I met *Bile* on my way to meet *Banba* for the first time. I have subsequently learned that *Bile* is not just the name of one sacred tree, but all sacred trees. In early times, these 'sacred' trees were often associated with Irish royal inauguration sites. They appear to have played an important part in Irish kingship ceremonies and as a result have been targeted by rival dynasties and even cut down.

Often the trees would be hazel. In ancient times, it was an important source of nutrition, year after year, and was a major mainstay in the diet of the day. Many trees that were held in reverence would usually refer to the usefulness of their properties. Even today, especially for True Believers, these trees remain sacred.

I empty my mind of everyday thoughts. I sit down by the ferns and absorb the life around me. I listen to hear the language of nature. I hear the voices of trees and birds, even insects.

Soon, there is a rustle in the leaves and there, in between two trees, facing me, is *Banba*.

"Greetings sister," she smiles as her shape slowly becomes clearer. "I have brought a fellow being to meet you."

I hear a movement from the direction I have just travelled. I turn and hear Epona make a slight whinny. I feel a presence behind me. It exudes safety and strength. I hear a voice in the whispers of the breeze through the trees.

Even before I turn to look, I can see and sense a golden aura behind me. It's as if the brightness of the day is bringing a new vivid essence to the green and brown shades of the forest. It's the brightness of a fresh page in my life. The kind that brings a smile even before you see it.

I turn. The brilliance facing me has kindled something beautiful within me. It's stirred a connection with the nature around me. Epona senses it too. She is still and unafraid. It's one of those days. The soul of the being behind me is so vibrant it begins to merge with every living thing, radiating warmth which resonates in the air, elevating my spirit.

It's *Epona.* The goddess ! She stands before me in all her glory. She nuzzles my horse and then turns to me.

"Hello young Aoife."

I am speechless and thrilled. She is as I imagined, but better. She appears as a centaur, a creature from Greek mythology, with the upper body of a human and the lower body and legs of a palomino horse. Her hair is her flowing mane, long and settling in waves on her neck and back.

Mam had told me that this half-human, half-horse composition is called a 'liminal' being. They have dual natures. They are both the embodiment of untamed nature, yet conversely, teachers and advisers.

One of my favourite authors since I was younger, is C.S. Lewis. His Chronicles of Narnia series depicts what he describes as centaurs, as the wisest and noblest of creatures. Narnian Centaurs are gifted at stargazing, prophecy, healing, and warfare. They are a fierce and valiant race always faithful to the High King, Aslan the Lion.

All these thoughts tumble into my mind as I stand up and remain glued to the spot, not quite sure of how to respond. In the end, I just take a deep breath and release her name, "*Epona,* " on my outgoing breath.

I stand closer to my own horse. She gives me comfort and I sense she feels no danger in the presence of this goddess.

"Do not be afraid, young friend. *Banba* has told me of your love for your horse. I have watched you and see you are becoming an experienced rider. You and your horse, who bears my name, are a good team."

"Thank you," I answer shyly.

"I know you have read about me. I can bring dreams to you. I can help you to improve your riding until you are the best of your kind." She pauses. "I can help you manifest your dreams if you allow me to accompany you on your path."

"I would be honoured, as would Epona." I indicate my horse."

"Horses are such a part of you, I know you are empathetic. Would you ride with me ?"

I am overwhelmed. I think of how this mystical goddess is revered. Her beauty, her speed, her bravery and her energy. She wants me to ride with her !

All I can do is nod.

"It shall be just before dawn tomorrow. Find the place where two roads cross each other. They must be perfectly oriented to the four directions: North, South, East and West. You will light eight small fires, one for each side of the roads and be sure to leave enough room for a horse and rider to pass through. Wait for me and we shall begin by riding three times around the intersection on a besom and then our fun will begin."

I know that a besom is an old word for a broom made of twigs, tied round a stick.

"Where will we go ?"

"I shall have spent the night dispensing dreams and nightmares, depending on the good or bad behaviour of the recipients."

That does sound scary.

She reads my thoughts. "Be not afraid. There is nothing bad for you. Be early. Sit and wait for me. We shall travel West, away from the approaching rays of morning."

I nod agreement.

"Remember, I am the protector of horses and riders and their mounts. I guard my devotees, like you, throughout their lives and into the Otherworld. At another level, I reflect the deep mysteries of life, death and rebirth."

I make a mental note to create a niche in our stable for a shrine to the goddess *Epona*. Tucked into a curve on the main wooden post that supports the main beam of the stable would be a perfect place. I will decorate it with freshly gathered flowers. I don't know why I haven't thought of it before.

Before I can say more, *Epona* begins to vanish. She becomes a cloud, The cloud spreads through the forest, creating a grey and silver form of light. For a few moments, the trees of every hue are cloaked in white velvet. The dampness of the cloud feeds the forest. It clears the air and refreshes the river. With her forest cloud, it's as though *Epona* has come as an artist to repaint a fresh three-dimensional canvas.

Banba smiles. "You are honoured, Aoife." She floats away raising her hand in salute as she leaves me.

We pause together for a moment. Then, I loosen Epona's reins and, using a sturdy branch, I remount.

We turn for home. Epona senses my excitement and increases her speed accordingly. We gallop, joined as one like our Goddess protector. The rhythm of the gallop is the drumbeat of my heart. Epona flies on spirit, not feet. Galloping free and wild.

When I return to the paddock, Mam is waiting. She smiles knowingly.

"Tomorrow, we must set the alarm clock," is all she says.

"As soon as we reach the house, I dash up to Da's library to see what else I can find about the Goddess *Epona*.

Mam appears with a glass of lemonade for me. She leaves me to it.

I soon get lost in reading. Apparently, sculptural depictions of *Epona* bear out what Da told me about her connections with fertility. There are several pictures of her in human form flanked by ponies, or with a mare and foal.

In one statuette the figure of *Epona* offers corn to the horses from a cornucopia . One relief shows her seated along with triads of horses and the sacrifice of a pig (yuk !) which is recognised as another symbol of fertility. Another relief, from Germany, shows the mounted goddess holding a round object which looks like a fruit – the cornucopia again – the idea of feeding the horses.

In Celtic culture, *Epona* is connected with ideas about the Otherworld. This magical supernatural realm is the source of our Celtic wisdom. It is, of course, the place of our gods and goddesses. It's the dimension in which poets and travellers are most at home. Whoever has visited the Otherworld, or formed a relationship with those supernatural beings, becomes more than mortal. The Otherworld is generally understood to lie close to the borders of the Earthly world and yet be light years away, simultaneously.

In some of the ancient stories, it lies within the compass of one ship sailing to the islands of the furthest West beyond Ireland. Maybe the Americas ? I have read that there are many links between the American Indians' and the Celts' beliefs. Back in the 19th century, many Irish people travelled to America in the hope of a better life, especially during the so-called famine of the 1850s where the Irish were starved and thrown out of their home by cruel English landlords. All the food produced at that time was taken and sent to England, so the Irish went hungry and thousands died. Those who were lucky enough to reach America met and formed close bonds with the American Indians, who, like them, had been ill-treated by Europeans who landed and claimed the land which had belonged to the Indians for millennia.

Back to *Epona*. She is frequently depicted as a woman sitting side-saddle, facing right, on a horse that is moving at a leisurely pace, walking, not galloping. *Epona*'s posture may connect with the ritual right hand turn which ensured good fortune.

The mare that carries her is part of her identity; sometimes separate and sometimes appearing as I saw her, a variation on conjoined twins.

Epona has also been connected with death, and there is evidence of *Epona* in cemetery plaques and monuments.

A cemetery at Metz in France, which was once the capital of the Mediomatrici tribe around the first century BC, has several monuments to *Epona*. One of them depicts *Epona* riding her mare and leading a human to the Otherworld.

The fragment of a lintel from Nages, Gard, in France, is decorated with two severed human heads and two galloping horses, which are believed to suggest *Epona*'s cult.

Epona is also linked in myth to other Celtic goddesses. For instance, *Rhiannon* appears in Welsh mythology, riding on a white horse. Her name comes from *'Rigantona'* meaning 'great, divine, queen'. Although she rides slowly, no-one can catch up with her.

Epona has had many meanings over time, but first and foremost she is a divine woman riding on a mare. Her swiftness and beauty, her supernatural power, linked with fertility and tribal territory, make her a formidable goddess who when being part of, or riding her horse, represents a path to the Otherworld.

I hope that she will point the path intended for me. *Aoife* has already told me that my future is full of possibilities and I should always remain open-minded and be prepared to invite new choices into my life. I am so lucky to have met these three goddesses. I shall treasure my relationship with them. I know they will guide me well.

Aoife once told me that I shall be victorious in my efforts if I concentrate on goodness.

The night before my ride with *Epona, Aoife* visits me. She tells me she will follow my ride, ensure my safety and is happy for me in my joy over the opportunity for such a fantastical experience.

As she arrives, a thunderstorm appears. The sky turns a molten silver. The sky and the Earth blend into one, cocooned in darkness. A percussion of rain crashes down on the rooftop.

"I have a story for you. You may know a version from your earlier childhood." *Aoife* began to sing.

I love singing. I'm not a good singer, but singing, or listening to song, has a way of releasing emotions held within. *Aoife* has a heavenly voice. She has sung lullabies to me in times when I couldn't sleep. Her singing gives the words of a song the emotions that gave them their soul when they were written. If I think back to bards and minstrels of long ago, I realise how much their words, in song or verse, communicate not just stories, but the emotions involved. I am sure that song must have existed in this world long before we had words to put to the tunes. As such, the songs always say so much more in the air, than they ever could as ink and paper.

Aoife begins. Her voice floats in the air.

> *"Ride a cock-horse to Banbury Cross,*
> *To see a fine lady upon a white horse;*
> *Rings on her fingers and bells on her toes,*
> *And she shall have music wherever she goes."*

I clap gently. She smiles.

I recognise the well-known nursery rhyme connected to the town of Banbury, in Oxfordshire, The lady on horseback evokes a powerful horse-woman. There are a number of suggestions as to the origin of the story. Banbury is in an area occupied by the Celtic *Brigantes* tribe and this could be the link to the well-known folk tale of Lady Godiva. In one story, Lady Godiva rode naked through a town, now modern Coventry, also in *Brigantes* territory. Her extremely long hair was her only covering. Legend says that she did it to shame her husband into lifting onerous taxes on the ordinary people. She apparently blinded a 'peeping tom' ! Her significance as a powerful horsewoman may well connect with devotees of the goddess *Epona*.

We sing the song together this time. Then, the thunderstorm abates. *Aoife* gently leans over and kisses my forehead. She disappears into a soft mist and is gone.

I lie back on my pillow, ready for sleep. Singing has brought my soul into alignment with the vibrations of the universe.

The statue of the 'fine lady' at Banbury.

(18) The Ride at Dawn

Date; 1969

> *All in green went my love riding*
> *on a great horse of gold*
> *into the silver dawn.*

(E.E. Cummings -1894 -1962 - American poet, painter, essayist, author, and playwright.)

Mam creeps into my room while it's still dark. She places a cup of tea by my bedside and shakes me gently.

"It's time," she whispers.

I wake with a start and sit up quickly. I feel as if there is an explosion in my brain. A good one. The sort that carries more possibilities than I can imagine. Hundreds of ideas fizz round in a buzz of electricity.

I can feel the calling card of adventure ! Uncharted paths awaiting. Whatever's ahead will be a great challenge. There could be tears before bedtime, but it's my adventure to take. Mam knows that. She says nothing. She just smiles.

I climb out of bed. Washing and dressing is done in a daze. The adventure to come is like a song in my head that whispers to my soul, telling of new things upon the horizon.

I can't eat breakfast because I'm too excited, so Mam and I make our way to the stable. Epona is ready. She knows too. Just before dawn she and I set off and leave Mam waving behind us.

Last night, Mam and I had returned to the crossroads and laid the eight fires. Luckily rain wasn't forecast, so the kindling and wood will have remained dry. Next to a bush nearby, I had placed the besom.

I feel in my pocket to check for the nth time that I have the box of matches.

Epona and I set off.

Upon our arrival, I wait for the sun to appear over the horizon. Then, I light the fires. I have placed them along the edges of the tracks, in the open, away from trees and bushes. There is plenty of room for a horse and rider to pass through, as instructed by *Epona*. I watch as the sparks leap in the air. The fires have taken well and as they burn, they have the appearance of flickering piles of gold.

I look round waiting to see what happens next. *Epona*'s words run through my head. "You will light eight small fires, one for each side of the roads and be sure to leave enough room Wait for me and we shall begin by riding three times around the intersection on a besom and then our fun will begin."

I watch as the dawn ignites the green protectors of the tracks. The boughs of the oaks arc into the light, standing firm as if on sentry duty, each one rooted into the earth.

Dawn brings a sunlight crown, smiling upward at dark heavens. The passing night and I welcome her more with each minute.

By dawn's early light, I hear the sound of distant hooves. My heart leaps. I watch intently to the East. I see dust rising. Then the magical horse comes into sight, flying above the path. At this moment, the sun opens up like a flower on the horizon behind the creature, offering a golden halo to the heavens. The sun sends petals of gold to warm and bless the forest, its leaves, branches and roots.

As *Epona* glides along, I sense that she is a divine agent , here to restore the Earth and its creations for another day. She is one of those deities who can help to set humankind back onto a sustainable path of happiness and love. Her mission is a worthy one. Nevertheless, I am aware, that it can be difficult to bring love and safety concurrently in such a dangerous world.

She hardly seems to slow and then she is by my side. My own mount seems quite at ease with this Otherworldly being. I see her looking at the fires. She turns her head to me.

"You have done well, young Aoife. "

I show her the besom. She nods.

"Remember I said that we shall begin by riding three times around the intersection on the besom and then our fun will begin."

"Yes", I say excitedly.

To my further amazement, *Epona* now metamorphoses into a young woman. She is holding the mane of her horse, who seems quite unperturbed by the change.

"Leave the mounts here. Bring the besom. As we stand together she instructs me to straddle the besom behind her as she does the same. I can't help feeling like a witch on a broomstick !

Together on the besom we resemble a fantastical creature. *Epona* spreads her arms like wings and tells me to do the same. We open our wings wide and fly heavenward through the growing light of day. We are like birds in the sky, flowing like music for the eyes, moving together in a choreographed melody.

We fly through the spreading canvas of the dawn. I swear I can see feathers on my arms. They feel buoyant just like a bird's wings. I know that these wings in this sky today will remain in my dreams and whenever I need a memory to lift me off the ground, they will be there.

Finally, to my disappointment we land.

"That was fun was it not ?" *Epona* asks.

I give a breathless, "yes".

"Now we can mount our steeds and fly," she instructs me. I am afraid that my Epona will be spooked, but *Epona* reads my mind and reassures me. Feeling as light as air, I am able to rise up and mount my horse without the help of hand or branch.

The manes of our horses sparkle in the light of the rising sun. Without me doing anything, we rise upward together. Soon we are in full flight. We sit up and raise our heads to the sun. I watch as the bright light refracts into brilliant rainbow beams.

Below us is the quenched grassland and the trees of the forest with their branches looking up as if they are following our path.

As I watch *Epona* alongside me, it was as if each second of time had expanded. Maybe time itself had expanded. It was as if the horses were in slow motion, yet travelling fast and far. I watch in amazement as *Epona*'s golden mane, twisted to form what appeared as the trunk of a tree. Wispy ends protruded, grew and became branches stretching outwards into infinity. Despite the change, *Epona* remained a vision of golden agility, with the tree perfectly balanced on her equine head.

All too soon, the magical journey comes to an end. *Epona*'s body reverts to girl and horse. I knew we were returning to the earth. The aerial view has leant me a new sense of perspective that only distance may provide. There below me is everything that matters to me. My home, the land, the castle, all woven into a tapestry of buildings set in green grassland and brown forest. It is far away, yet somehow closer than before. It is a world without frontiers from the sky above. It has a language all its own. Beyond mere words.

Finally, the clouds part to show a canvas of terra firma.

Epona is gone. Fleeter than if she had been a dream.

I find myself close to the paddock.. I lead Epona back towards the stable where I find Mam waiting. She looks at me enquiringly.

"Fabulous," is all I can manage. The experience is really indescribable.

Mam knows.

Together we go through the after ride care routine.

I had dismounted in the paddock, so that I could walk *Epona* back to the stable. Once inside I dismount. I offer her water which she drinks readily. Then Mam helps to hose her down. I feel her legs and pick out her hooves. She is in good fettle.

Mam and I walk back to the house arm in arm. When we return, Da is coming out of the kitchen with a pot of tea. The table's laid with sandwiches and what smalls invitingly like newly baked scones.

I feel as if I've only been away for an hour or so, but when I consult the grandfather clock in the corner, it's nearly 5pm.

We all sit down and help ourselves to egg and cress and cheese and pickle sandwiches. Da's a dab hand at making bread and it's always soft and crusty. After the plates are emptied, we set to on the still warm scones, accompanied by homemade blackberry jam and thick cream.

Da utters his favourite expression at the table, "let your food, shut your gob !"

It's quite unnecessary, as we're focussed on eating. The food is swilled down by strong 'builders' tea.

There's a comfortable silence. I expect Mam and Da may have seen me flying over, even if it was in their heads.

We sit in silence for a while, enjoying the moment.

Da's the first to speak. " We can all feel the flow of future-time, because the deities communicate it to us. It's what we need to comprehend what comes and is to come. This is done in a way that prevents them from altering our timeline...."

"at least, only a little bit ! " Mam winks at me.

"Da nods. "It's just enough to bring about the best result possible. In this way they all act like a team, yet they also act independently. "

As I expected, *Aoife* returned that night. I had drifted off to sleep and I might have thought she had arrived in a dream, but the swish of her fine, feathery dress and the brightness in the room alerted me to her presence. She whispers, as if not to disturb me.

"*Epona* has told me to pass on the message that you have achieved the status of angel warrior. You are now armed with charms. If you see harm to being or beast, you can cure it with words, with spells that she will bring to you. The universe accepts you and co-ordinates with you to bring maximum good results to all the events in your life."

This sounds amazing. I am now fully awake and sit up to face *Aoife*.

"You overcame your fear on the journey that you undertook. That is a start to win hearts and souls in a way that is impossible for demons or devils to counter. *Epona* whispered words of love into the wind whilst you rode. These are spread in the form of healthy seeds planted in fertile soil. *Banba* fertilises the seeds with water. I shall bring the sunlight to them.

You will continue to develop as active and creative. You are gaining the strength to meet life's challenges. You will be a leader. You will take on responsibility, to rise and become a guardian. We shall continue to bring you a direct connection to love.. Do love and protect those you meet. Have patience with them because they may be wild sparks unaccustomed to considering others. Give them tolerance and respect. This will be your future. Best of fortune go with you child."

I feel blessed. It's a big responsibility, but I plan to do my best.

---

(19) The Moonstone

Giant steps are what you take
Walking on the moon
I hope my leg don't break
Walking on the moon
We could walk forever
Walking on the moon
We could live together
Walking on, walking on the moon
Walking back from your house
Walking on the moon
Walking back from your house
Walking on the moon
Feet they hardly touch the ground
Walking on the moon
My feet don't hardly make no sound
Walking on, walking on the moon

Some may say
I'm wishing my days away
No way
And if it's the price I pay
Some say
Tomorrow's another day
You stay
I may as well play
Giant steps are what you take
Walking on the moon
I hope my leg don't break
Walking on the moon
We could walk forever
Walking on the moon
We could be together
Walking on, walking on the moon
Some may say
I'm wishing my days away
No way
And if it's the price I pay
Some say
Tomorrow's another day
You stay
I may as well play
Keep it up, keep it up……

(Walking on the Moon – song by The Police – 1979)

Date 2021

In 1969, I was, as many around the world, glued to our black and white television to watch the Moon landing. I was sure the crew might meet supernatural beings, but no mention of greeting aliens was ever mentioned – officially anyway.

Twenty years ago, in 2001, what is claimed to be the oldest map of the moon ever made and situated in Ireland, was visited by two paleontologists. It is reached via a narrow triangular-shaped crack in the rock of an ancient Neolithic burial mound at Knowth in County Meath.

The two men edged towards the heart of the burial mound, hoping to uncover more of the mound's mysteries.
The complex was constructed around 3000 BC and is the largest and most remarkable ancient monument in Ireland. It has turned out to be an incredible treasure trove of stone engravings and artefacts. It also has the largest collection of megalithic art in Europe, consisting of strange circular and spiral patterns. Many people believe the ancient carvings to be lunar symbols.

The mound has two passages, one facing East and one facing West. They are the longest 'cairn' passages in Europe and are difficult to crawl through.

Once the men had reached the end of the narrow passage, it opened into the heart of this vast ancient burial mound - a tall, central chamber. In there is to be found a most intriguing mystery.

Until then, no-one thought that anyone had drawn the moon before Leonardo da Vinci's sketch, which was completed around 1505. The investigations in the burial mound revealed ancient rock carvings and also something else amazing. The markings in the burial chamber could be placed over a picture of the full moon and the two would line up !

The burial chamber carvings were without doubt a map of the moon, the most ancient one ever found. But few people, not even the archaeologists who discovered it, had seen the moonstone for real.

If that wasn't amazing enough, in one of four recesses that protrude from the main chamber, on a rock at the back, were markings on its surface. They had been made by 'pitting' the rock with a lump of quartz. Apparently, the pattern was hard to detect until a torch was gently swung back-and-fro in front of it.

The shape carved into the rock then seemed familiar. Dips and crevices which resemble the dark spots that can be seen on the moon with the naked eye, were visible. Was it a map of the moon ? Certainly, they found there is another map of the moon in one of the other recesses. In the recess was a large stone basin thought to be where the cremated remains of a local chieftain had been placed. The wall behind the basin astonished them. There can be seen clearly stars and crescents, undoubtedly images of the moon.

Some archaeologists wonder if the passages that reach into the central chamber allow sunlight, and moonlight, to shine down the passage into the central chamber at certain times. If this was the case, there would have been times at which moonlight would have shone on the back stone of the Eastern passage, lighting up a map of itself.

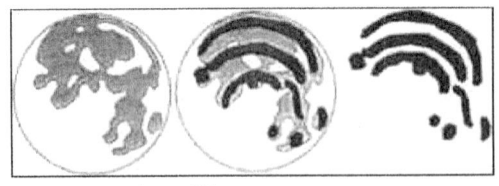

The ancient markings set over a modern Moon map

There is much speculation, but I know more. Here's the story:

Date: August 1969

Apollo 11 launched from Cape Kennedy on July 16, 1969, carrying Commander Neil Armstrong, Command Module Pilot Michael Collins and Lunar Module Pilot Edwin "Buzz" Aldrin into an initial Earth orbit of 114 by 116 miles.

It's been estimated that 650 million people watched Armstrong's televised image and heard his voice describe the event as he took "...one small step for a man, one giant leap for mankind" on July 20, 1969.

I am in my room, reading more about the Moon landing, I become aware of a familiar mist dancing on and around the mantelpiece. Cocooned within it is *Faoladh.*

He appears in his wolf form and is standing upright, holding out a paw in greeting from the mist that hugs his body. The cloud swirls around him like a comforting blanket moving serenely.

"Good evening, Aoife." His voice sounds human, yet, I can detect a slight howling tone behind it.

I find myself smiling. I am so happy to see him and full of anticipation. In that eureka moment of my spirit lifting, *Faoladh* give me a real Cheshire grin. Can a wolf grin like a cat ? The Cheshire Cat has the ability to become invisible and intangible. He can also teleport with his arrival being a secret due to his invisibility. Sounds familiar. Anyway I am always happy, in that rush of realisation, that my lupine friend is here.

Cheshire cat or grinning wolf ?

The mist dissipates and gradually *Faoladh's* form becomes a boy. I notice he is a little older than when I first saw him. Now around my age again !

"The Moon," he states.

My stomach does somersaults ! Do I know what's coming ?

He descends gently to the floor and takes my hand. "Come on then."

I grasp his hand willingly. We float away together, as if in a magical daydream.

Are we really going to the Moon ?" I ask.

"Of course," replies my companion. "You know by now, dear one, that there are infinite possibilities because your sentient life has free will. This is what you desire and through me such a journey is possible. You know, as a True Believer, that we and you, have a view of life free of your Earthly timeline. Possibilities lie across the Multiverse and throughout creation. You will return safely to the same time and place. Have no fear."

"I trust you completely," I tell him.

He smiles the Cheshire cat smile again. "We of the Otherworld only give this information to one who will use it wisely with a pure heart and in a manner that they cannot transmit the ability to others unless it is seen fit. Those, like you, who are blessed in this way, cannot tell of it in any way that makes sense to others outside. It is a light in the darkness that only your eyes can see, by divine design. A simple way to think of it is that it is like a sixth sense of sorts."

I love the way, *Faoladh* explains such things. It seems so clear.

Faoladh continues. Many humans will only experience living in the moment. We help you to have need to think, to grow in psychological and spiritual maturity. This is essential if entry to the Otherworld and rebirth is to become an assured destiny."

We continue upward into the darkening sky. Stars appear. There's a full Moon. As I look down, the Earth below becomes smaller and more distant. As we fly upwards, the land and sea become blurred and soon disappear from sight as we travel beyond my planet. At the same time, my spirit is lifted and my heart grows lighter.

As I watch *Faoladh*, he is concentrating on our direction of flight, like a pilot in an aeroplane. I have complete faith in him and this gives me a sense of liberation. Everyday problems and worries have been left behind.

As I try to absorb my surroundings, I take mental photographs and store them in my memory for later viewing.

I watch in amazement as we approach our target.

"Make ready for a smooth landing," advises *Faoladh*.

The landscape of the Moon draws closer and becomes clearer. I steel myself, but as we approach, we glide towards the surface and land on what feels like soft ground.

Faoladh invites me to sit with him and gaze at our surroundings. The view is incredible. The Moon's surface is covered with dead volcanoes, impact craters, and lava flows. I know this from books I have read and the descriptions by the astronauts. I recognise that some of these are visible to the Earthly stargazer. I know they are oceans of a sort, but rather than water, they are made up of pools of hardened lava from the volcanoes.

"Look further," suggests *Faoladh*. "Beyond the surface."

I scour the sky and realise that the tiny speck I can see in the far distance is Earth, my home.

"How do you feel now you're here?"

"Light and calm," I sigh happily.

"You can see how small Earth is. The view from here puts your planet into perspective. We of the Otherworld know this. You can see now how, in the Multiverse, all life forms are just tiny dots composed of atoms. All these elements are temporary. Some last longer than others. Some will cease to exist. Others, like True Believers will be reborn. Whenever you are faced with troubles, imagine being here as you are now, seeing all with a different eye."

"I understand."

Faoladh nods wisely. He thinks to himself that Aoife is growing right now in every sense.

"One thing is constant. I will always be here in the Multiverse watching and protecting."

I smile gratefully.

We continue our exploration. I notice that the surface of the moon has several inches of dust. One of the astronauts, Buzz Aldrin, from the Moon landing, described it as being like talcum-power, mixed with pebbles. He said that later, when the dust was examined under a microscope, you could see it's made up of tiny, solidified droplets of vaporised rock resulting from extreme velocity impacts, He said that his term "magnificent desolation" referred in part to the achievement of being there, and in part to the "eons of lifelessness".
Mr Aldrin also described weightlessness as "one of the most fun and enjoyable, challenging and rewarding, experiences of spaceflight. Perhaps not too far from a trampoline, but without the springiness and instability," he said.

Reading my thoughts, *Faoladh* tells me, "Much of this dust has fallen to the Moon from the empty spaces between the planets over the last several billions years. It feels pretty soft, like the sand on your beaches. "

"I saw this in some of the pictures taken by the astronauts of their footprints on the Moon."

Faoladh goes into his incredible scientific knowledge mode. "The average composition of the lunar surface by weight is roughly 43% oxygen, 20% silicon, 19% magnesium, 10% iron, 3% calcium, 3% aluminum, 0.42% chromium, 0.18% titanium and 0.12% manganese. "

"I also read," I respond , "that there may be traces of water on the lunar surface that may have originated from deep underground."

A knowing smile crosses *Faoladh*'s face.

We walk some more. It's amazing. More and more rolling terrain. I remember reading that one of the astronauts, said that by slowly raising his arm until his gloved thumb stood upright, he found that his thumb could entirely blot the planet Earth from view. "One small gesture and the Earth was gone," he added. He said he was asked about his time on the Moon and whether it changed him in any way. He replied, "I can describe the majesty of the lunar mountains, the layers of volcanic lava or the beauty of the sparkling crystals in the rocks, but only an artist or poet could convey the true beauty of space."

We continue our exploration. My sense of discovery has been ignited. Being here on the Moon is a trip that has moulded me closer to *Faoladh*. I know that such a challenge will make a stronger version of me.

I look out into the infinity of space. I think about my loved ones so far away. Being here is wonderful, but I would miss Earth if I could not return. Alll those little things like the sound of rain, the rides on my horse and, of course, my family. I am born of Earth after all. I am a daughter of her soil. As great as it was to leave and have this adventure, nothing will be better than coming home.

I know *Faoladh* understands what I am thinking and feeling. This time on the Moon, has taught me how deep my love of my Mother Planet, Earth, will always be.

"Close your eyes," instructs *Faoladh*.

I obey.

I feel a strange force pulling my body up and away from the Moon. I know we are on our way back to Earth. *Faoladh* holds my hand tight.

It happens so fast, in the blink of an eye this time. We fly so fast that I can imagine us crashing into the ground with a huge thump. Just as I prepare myself for a hard bump, we suddenly slowly and softly land in my bedroom. I felt as light as a feather on the return journey and it only took seconds.

Faoladh stroked my cheek with the back of a furry paw. He floated up over the fireplace and was gone in a silver mist, which afterwards floated to the floor like tiny pieces of tinsel.

……………………………….

2021

The clearest links for the importance of The Moon for True Believers, Druids and Celtic people going way back in time, are with the Celtic calendar which is a compilation of pre-Christian Celtic systems of timekeeping. The Coligny calendar is a second century Celtic calendar, first discovered in 1897 in Coligny, France. It's what known as a 'lunisolar' calendar and has a 5 year cycle of 62 months. It attempted to synchronize the solar year and the lunar month. The common lunar year contained 354 or 355 days. It is this that has been used to reconstruct the ancient Celtic calendar, as we know it now. The letters on the calendar are in Latin and the language used is Gaulish. The calendar is used to define the beginning and length of the day, the week, the month, the seasons, quarter days, and festivals.

The calendar features 'weeks' of 5 days. Each month has 6 weeks and either 29 or 30 days. There are twelve such months in a year, making 354 days. A calendar cycle consists of 5 years of 60 regular months, plus 2 'intercalary' months.

The importance feature of the calendar is that it must remain in synch with the lunar phases. That means that the 5 year cycle is 1,831 days long.

However, this makes the calendar fall adrift from the seasons by almost a day every year. Roman sources suggest that the Celtic calendar has a 30 year cycle. That means that a month is 'lost' once every 30 years.

Each Celtic month starts on the 6th day of the lunar cycle, the date of the quarter moon, the easiest lunar date to confirm by direct observation from Earth. I can see how this ties in with the importance of the ancient Moon map.

Da explained to me many years ago that the Modern Druidic Calendar is based on the same form.

The Druids were renowned in the classical world for their knowledge of astronomy and astrology. This has lasted into modern times.

To the Celts and to those of the Otherworld, time is circular rather than linear. This is reflected in their beginning each day, and each festival, at dusk rather than dawn. It is also reflected in the year starting with the festival of *Samhain* on 31 October, when nature appears to be dying down. Tellingly, the first month of the Celtic year is *Samonios*, (Seed Fall), symbolising from death and darkness springs life and light.

Da also explained that another reason for the importance of night in the reckoning of time lies in True Believers' and those from The Otherworld's strong regard for the Moon and the feminine principles which it represents. It is also true that the Druids' most sacred plant, mistletoe, is associated with the Sun. However, the waxing and waning of the Moon is of far greater importance.

....

Date; 2nd November 1969

It was my 16th birthday yesterday. Mam and Da presented me with the most beautiful natural moonstone. It has a dazzling blue lustre and, most importantly, a flickering inside which Da told me is called 'irisation'.

He explained, "the moonstone absorbs light during the day and glows for up to 3 hours into the night."

I can't help touching and stroking its surface.

Da added, "one of the most fascinating moonstone facts is that they have healing properties. These characteristics are due to the unique vibrational frequency that each gem possesses due to its original formation process. It's said that if you place the gem near your bed or even under the mattress, it will keep you calm and less fearful of the unknown."

"That's amazing. I'll keep it on my bedside table, so that I can watch the glow."

Mam told me more. "The moonstone can help with lots of ailments.

"Such as ?" I want to know.

"It keeps a balance in your emotional state. Good for teenage angst," she laughs.

I make a face.

"It's also said to inspire passion, creativity, and a sense of direction in one's life. It helps you relax, accept what happens in your everyday life and opens up your intuition." She pauses.

"Oh yes. It helps you to make wise decisions and increases your confidence. "

Da continues. "The healing power of Moonstones has been known since ancient times, It is also thought to give the wearer the ability to predict the future !"

Wow ! I thought. "How can it do that ?"

Da said, "see the way the stone is shallower at one end ?"

I nod.

"It's suggested that you place at least part of the Moonstone in your mouth during a full Moon. It's believed that the Moon's gravitational pull and its ability to coax the energy from the stone will do the trick !"

They both admitted that they hadn't tried it.

Mam said, " it's also said to be the Bringer of Good Fortune as well as its healing properties."

Now I'm in my bedroom, I put down my pen and my journal and hold the Moonstone carefully in my hand, feeling into all its nooks and crannies. I then put my hand to my neck. As well as the stone, Mam and Da gave me a lovely polished Moonstone set in a silver frame and hung on a silver chain. I shall never take it off. Mam has one like it and she wears it always.

I know that since ancient times, Moonstones have been used to create elegant necklaces, bracelets, and other ornamental jewellery.

When Mam and I were alone when I went to bed last night, she also told me that Moonstone is considered feminine in nature. The lunar cycle controls a woman's monthly cycle and the Moonstone can help with the horrible side effects such as premenstrual pain. She also said that she used the help of her Moonstone when she was pregnant with me and during childbirth. She believed it helped.

…………………………..

I later read that one of the other fascinating Moonstone facts is that the Moon landings elevated the Moonstone to the status of the Florida State Gemstone. That's because the Kennedy Space Centre is in Florida and it also celebrated NASA's achievements.

I also did more reading about Moonstones' qualities. One of the most interesting has to do with appearance is the gem's 'adularescent' qualities. Adularescence refers to the rippling blue light that appears when you turn the Moonstone round and round near a source of light. This effect is due to the interwoven properties of a separate 'feldspar' (a mineral) in varying positions inside the moonstone. It's a bit like a cat's eye. When a strand of light seems to linger over the Moonstone as you rotate it, the appearance is like a cat's alert eye.

Another quality is called 'asterism'. It's quite rare and refers to the image of a star on the exterior of the gem. As light filters in, the star can change shape or size.

Moonstone gems have also been used in many supernatural stories. Most often in stories about vampires or werewolves. Moonstones are believed to have the ability to either enhance or suppress the abilities of supernatural creatures. Interesting !

Natural Moonstone

Polished Moonstone

There is also a sacred meaning to the Moonstone. Seen as a veiled spectacle of light, or cirrus clouds, passing over the Moon, it's said to form a link with the Otherworld and its beings. The pearly iridescence is such a thing of beauty, it holds a deep meaning. It's why it's highly valued by monks, shamans, spiritualists, and believers from many religions.

As ancient as the Moon itself, the meaning of Moonstone lies within its energy. Together with the waxing and waning of the moon, it evokes tranquillity of a sensual, esoteric nature. It gives off a glowing vitality that can re-energise the mind and body and wash negativity away. Since it is enveloped by strong rays of gold, blue, and purple, Moonstone is perpetually embraced with gleaming white energy that makes it a protective gem.

I love my Moonstones and will treasure them for ever.

_____

(20) A View of Mother Ireland

Date: 2021

All of the Otherworld females which I have come across, in The Ether, or in stories, have had characteristics which give them a roundness which makes them believable female prototypes. Like my Otherworld sister, *Aoife*, She is strong, even war-like, when she feels she needs to be. Yet, she has been loving and protective to me when circumstances demanded. She allowed me to reinvent myself in other forms when I was younger, in order to give me a view of my past in order to widen my view of all the possibilities this present life can offer.

Some argue that myth is only significant as long as it is relevant to the context it exists in. Myth is an integral part of life, but only endures as long as it is important to a particular society. However, it is difficult to dismiss the numerous examples of Irish mythological heroines such as *Aoife, Banba, Epona, Macha* and others, and call them just inventions. There are elements of the original stories which have undeniably been altered to suit Christian beliefs. Many would call me ungodly, or simply potty ! It's a question of existing in a wider universe, outside of time or place, and accepting it as natural. Living without my sisters and or being outside our Earthly world would be a much narrower existence. Maybe simpler, but I wouldn't do without it !

Christian interpreters have, no doubt, used the myths to serve their own purposes in their own context, and shaped them as they thought fit, but some original myths and the characters within them, do survive. Not only do they give a fascinating glimpse of a rich, literary, pre-Christian past, but continue in a very real sense. I can attest to this personally.

My Otherworldly sisters and those Earthly sisters of family members are strong women. They exhibit protective natures, but there are examples where, like humans, they have proved fallible, dual-natured. In certain circumstances, sisters, from wherever, may not see eye to eye. It's then down to each individual's conscience to follow the path they feel is right.

Another interesting case for the elevated status of ancient Celtic women is found in their surprisingly progressive early codes of law. Children had status and worth. They also had the opportunity for education, with no discrimination against gender. Children were to be brought up by both parents. Although, if a child was a product of rape, the child had to be the responsibility of the man alone. (not sure I like that idea !)

Most importantly, however, was the woman's eligibility to inherit property, retain the wealth she brought into a marriage, take part in the military and political activities of the clan, divorce, engage in polygamy (!) and to seek recourse for rape or assault.

This status also brought with it the fact that women had to take responsibility for their own behaviour. For example, they had to face the same punishment as a man for murder.

Interestingly, as Christianity began spreading into Ireland, laws against prostitution were introduced. This was at a time when the profession of 'ladies of the night', was expanding, most likely due to the change from polygamous relationships, which were restricted by the Church, to monogamous relationships. There was also a new importance on a woman's state of virginity before marriage introduced by the Church.

Those who lived in goddess-worshipping cultures assumed that such deities existed alongside and within Earthly communities. They were separate, but also one. This ties in with the triune idea – also used in Christianity as God being three in one – father, son and holy spirit – presumably all men.

Relationships between men and women, therefore, in particular the power balance, was very different from what it became in later patriarchal societies.

I wasn't aware of this as a girl, but much has been written in more recent times about the possibility of certain goddesses being violent by nature. It has been suggested that some all-female societies were extremely violent and cruel. Was this simply a single facet of their personalities, or were they indeed, like us, dual-natured ?

In modern Irish literature, my favourite Irish poet, WB Yeats (1865 - 1939) wrote about the dual-natured mother/warrior-goddess at her most terrifying. The goddess, as a female, is essential to the Natural world and the cycle of birth, life and death. If such beings are destroyers, he argues, we have the unwelcome cycle of birth, violent life and brutal death repeating itself for eternity. A very negative view to say the least !

W.B. Yeats – 1865 – 1939) (Irish poet, dramatist and prose writer)

Yet, Yeats spoke of 'Mother Ireland', a personification of the concept of the protectress as she appears in the 20th century. She is still a warrior and too much blood has been shed during her history. Yeats asks the question, "Is there anything in Ireland worth saving? " Is he suggesting that because, at a particular point in history, Ireland rejected the matri-centred, goddess-honouring society, it must reap the consequences of Christianity and patriarchy ?

Morrigan, on the other hand, is a different goddess, known as the goddess of war. Her name is translated as "Great Queen," "Phantom Queen" or "Queen of Demons." She was believed to hover over a battlefield in the form of either a crow or a raven, and supposedly influenced or predicted the outcome of the battle.

Of course, it's far more complex than that and, as I've indicated before, change was gradual. Interpretations of these supernatural beings and their qualities and behaviour have metamorphosed over centuries, even millennia.

Symbolically, poets like Yeats blame Mother Ireland for the bloodshed carried out in her name. In her is the very heart of Ireland. These writers lament the slaughter of battle. They are disgusted by the female warrior ethos. They love her, fear her and blame her. I see in their words how the earlier idea of the courageous and chivalrous female warrior has been turned on its head.

When he was a young man, Yeats began his interest in occultism. This was interpreted as an study and involvement in all the arts and sciences of the occult - alchemy, astrology, magic, divination and occult medicine. The occult relates to the nature of secrets which are often, or usually, invisible to most human non-believers. I haven't found out whether Yeats had these experiences himself. He may have balked at making that knowledge public considering the era in which he lived.

Fans of W. B. Yeats' work often disagree whether he could have believed in what is strangest in his work. I think there seems to be a collaboration between him and his wife. He writes about entities not of this Earthly plane of being. However, he speaks of them as if he believed they were external to consciousness and only when we enter into the dream world is there is a dramatic split or separation of what he calls 'ego' - the self, especially as contrasted with another self or the world.

Yeats believed that while we dream, we are persuaded of the existence of unknown people or beings, which, when we wake up, we feel were only part of our own nature. He compares this with the characteristics of Proteus. In Greek mythology, Proteus is the prophetic old man of the sea. He is a shepherd of the sea's creatures. He had a varied nature and the ability to assume different forms. He was subject to the sea god Poseidon. These entities communicated to the poet and his wife in visions. Yeats may have believed this was simply a submerged part of the soul. I know better !

Yeats also met John O'Leary, a famous patriot who had returned to Ireland after 20 years of imprisonment and exile for revolutionary nationalistic activities. O'Leary had a keen enthusiasm for Irish books, music, and ballads, and he encouraged young writers like Yeats to adopt Irish subjects. Until then, Yeats, with the romanticism of youth, had preferred more romantic settings and themes. He soon took O'Leary's advice and began to produce poems based on Irish legends, folklore, ballads and songs.

In London, he met Maud Gonne (1866 – 1953). In Irish, her name was *Nic Ghoinn Bean Mhic Giolla Bhríghde.* She was a tall, beautiful young woman who mixed in high society. She was passionately devoted to Irish nationalism. Although English-born she was very much an Irish Republican revolutionary. She was also a suffragette and actress.

_Maud Gonne

Maud shared Yeats's interest in occultism and spiritualism. He was a theosophist. The term theosophy is derived from the Greek 'theos', meaning god and 'Sophia' meaning wisdom. It's generally understood to mean 'divine wisdom'. In 1890, he turned from its mystical insights and joined the 'Golden Dawn', a secret society that practiced ritual magic. He remained an active member of the Golden Dawn for 32 years, becoming involved in its development . He achieved the coveted sixth grade of membership in 1914. That same year, his future wife, Georgiana Hyde-Lees, also joined the society.

Although Yeats' occult ambitions were a powerful force in his private thoughts, the Golden Dawn's emphasis on the supernatural clashed with his own need as a poet for interaction in the physical world.

Yeats experimented with occult symbolism in his work. As an example, in his 1899 collection entitled 'The Wind Among The Reeds', he used this genre in several poems.

Most of Yeats' poetry, however, used symbols from ordinary life and from familiar traditions. Much of his poetry in the 1890s continued to reflect his interest in Irish subjects.

The turn of the century marked Yeats' increased interest in theatre, an interest influenced by his father, a famed artist and orator, who loved highly dramatic moments in literature. In 1904, his play, 'On Baile's Strand' was performed in Dublin. It was the first of his several plays featuring the heroic ancient Irish warrior *Cuchulain*. This is a character I know well from my own reading and experience. My journal includes the stories from his life.

The Easter Rising contributed to Yeats's eventual decision to reside in Ireland rather than England, and his marriage to Georgie Hyde-Lees in 1917 further strengthened that resolve.

Easter, 1916 – WB Yeats

I have met them at close of day
Coming with vivid faces
From counter or desk among grey
Eighteenth-century houses.
I have passed with a nod of the head
Or polite meaningless words,

*Or have lingered awhile and said
Polite meaningless words,
And thought before I had done
Of a mocking tale or a gibe
To please a companion
Around the fire at the club,
Being certain that they and I
But lived where motley is worn:
All changed, changed utterly:
A terrible beauty is born.*

*That woman's days were spent
In ignorant good-will,
Her nights in argument
Until her voice grew shrill.
What voice more sweet than hers
When, young and beautiful,
She rode to harriers?
This man had kept a school
And rode our wingèd horse;
This other his helper and friend
Was coming into his force;
He might have won fame in the end,
So sensitive his nature seemed,
So daring and sweet his thought.
This other man I had dreamed
A drunken, vainglorious lout.
He had done most bitter wrong
To some who are near my heart,
Yet I number him in the song;
He, too, has resigned his part
In the casual comedy;
He, too, has been changed in his turn,
Transformed utterly:
A terrible beauty is born.*

*Hearts with one purpose alone
Through summer and winter seem
Enchanted to a stone
To trouble the living stream.
The horse that comes from the road,
The rider, the birds that range
From cloud to tumbling cloud,
Minute by minute they change;
A shadow of cloud on the stream
Changes minute by minute;*

A horse-hoof slides on the brim,
And a horse plashes within it;
The long-legged moor-hens dive,
And hens to moor-cocks call;
Minute by minute they live:
The stone's in the midst of all.

Too long a sacrifice
Can make a stone of the heart.
O when may it suffice?
That is Heaven's part, our part
To murmur name upon name,
As a mother names her child
When sleep at last has come
On limbs that had run wild.
What is it but nightfall?
No, no, not night but death;
Was it needless death after all?
For England may keep faith
For all that is done and said.
We know their dream; enough
To know they dreamed and are dead;
And what if excess of love
Bewildered them till they died?
I write it out in a verse—
MacDonagh and MacBride
And Connolly and Pearse
Now and in time to be,
Wherever green is worn,
Are changed, changed utterly:
A terrible beauty is born.

In this poem, I see Yeats using the use of rich symbolism through colour, signs and sounds. Certain symbols bring to the fore associations with important events in the history of Ireland. The emotions associated to the 'Easter Uprising' are brought to life by rich symbolism. The colours affect our emotions through both things that we associate with them, as well as their preordained energies. The symbol of 'terrible beauty', 'the stone', and the colour 'green' evoke the emotions that Irish people would experience in the context of the story of the 'Easter Uprising' told in this form. The stone represents the strength and determination of those involved. I think the 'terrible beauty' is the struggle itself and the dreadful consequences. Although it's part of Irish history, it is thought to be preordained. Something that those in the Otherworld knew would happen, but did not interfere with.

Like most Irish people, I believe that the execution of the leaders of Irish Republican Brotherhood who rebelled against the British in their attempt to gain independence for Ireland, was barbaric. In his poem, Yeats evokes emotions of sorrow at the outcome of events, but sets that against feelings of pride and nationalism which are noble and beautiful. Chivalry and bravery again !

Yeats also suggests that 'woman' represents rebellion. It signifies and evokes emotions of the Irish rebellion. This is the female warrior in her dual-aspect form – aggressive but in a good cause.

Like Yeats, I have a fascination for the contrast between a person's internal and external self. Our true nature, or natures, as opposed to the self we present to others and the world in general.

Yeats continued to explore mysticism. After his wedding with Georgie, his bride began what would be a lengthy experiment with the psychic phenomenon called 'Automatic Writing'. Georgie had a paper and pen which she wanted to serve as unconscious instruments for the Spirit or Otherworld to send messages and information. After holding more than 400 sessions of Automatic Writing, Georgie produced nearly 4,000 pages ! Yeats then enthusiastically studied and organised the words. He used what was written to formulate theories about life and history. He came to recognise particular patterns which he called 'Gyres'. These were interlinked, representing mixtures of opposites, both personal and historical in nature. He argued that Gyres were initiated by the divine impregnation of a Human woman by a Supernatural being, perhaps a God. He gave examples from ancient stories. One being the rape of Leda by the God Zeus.

Leda and Zeus

In his poem 'Leda and the Swan' (the Swan again !) Yeats retells the classic Greek myth in which Leda, a human woman, is impregnated by the god Zeus while he is in the form of a swan. This conception results in the birth of Helen of Troy, who grows up to cause the legendary Trojan War ! This event is recognised as the catalyst for the Golden Age of Greece and the dawn of what we think of as modern history. In his compelling version of the myth, Yeats uses the sonnet form in such a way as to capture and illustrate the powerful forces by which history is made.

I find it interesting that in this story the woman is not honoured and she is the victim of the god. This would have seemed to fit with the perception of Earthly women's place in family and society at the early part of the 20th century, when Yeats was writing. Possibly also in ancient Greek culture ?

<u>Leda and the Swan by W.B. Yeats</u>

A sudden blow: the great wings beating still
Above the staggering girl, her thighs caressed
By the dark webs, her nape caught in his bill,
He holds her helpless breast upon his breast.

How can those terrified vague fingers push
The feathered glory from her loosening thighs?
And how can body, laid in that white rush,
But feel the strange heart beating where it lies?

A shudder in the loins engenders there
The broken wall, the burning roof and tower
And Agamemnon dead.
Being so caught up,
So mastered by the brute blood of the air,
Did she put on his knowledge with his power
Before the indifferent beak could let her drop?

Leda and the Swan depicts a violent act of rape. The graphic imagery Yeats' presents leaves no doubt. It lays bare the violence of Leda's rape and its equally brutal consequence, the Trojan War. However, it seems to be condoning violence leading to violence. I think the poem seems to revel in sensuality. This ambiguous depiction creates a central tension of the poem. It's left unresolved. The poet doesn't condemn or approve of Leda's rape. His focus is on the act as possibly being acceptable as it will have a huge mythological significance. Looking at it from a human woman's viewpoint, I would take issue with him about that ! However, in the Otherworld is the concept of morality different ? Is something bad necessary to initiate something good ? War being the obvious example. It's something which comes to light at different points in my life in my interaction with supernatural beings.

In Yeats' interpretation of the mythological tale, the opening phrase, "A sudden blow," suggests violence right away. Words such as "helpless," and "terrified" make it clear that Leda is taken by force. Leda's initial panic, confusion, and resistance upon being attacked are coherently expressed . She is fragile and therefore a victim. A human woman has no chance against the god Zeus disguised in his "feathered glory" and "white rush". Sensuality is conjured up by words and phrases like "thighs, "caressed," "nape," "holds her ... breast" and, later, "feathered glory" and "shudder in the loins". Could it suggest that her body cannot help but "feel the strange heart" of Zeus ?

In the end, I'm not sure if the poem is critical of the act by suggesting violence leading to more violence or is Yeats suggesting that the end is inevitable regardless of whether Zeus' act was rape or seduction ? It gets complicated !!

Yeats' research found that within each 2,000 year period, important, emblematic moments occurred at the midpoints of the 1000 year halves. At these moments of balance, he believed a civilisation could achieve a special level of excellence. He suggested examples like the magnificence of Athens in 500 B.C., Byzantium in A.D. 500, and the Italian Renaissance in A.D. 1500.

He suggested these historical cycles were like the 28-day lunar cycle. The moon's physical existence grows steadily until it reaches a maximum at the full moon, the most beautiful. In the remaining half of the cycle, physical existence gradually fades, until it disappears completely at the new moon. Then, the cycle begins again. This ties in with periods in history and the lives of individuals. Humans, animals and plants grow in phases as they change from birth to maturity, then old age and finally death. If, like Otherworld beings, we are reborn ad infinitum, we may grow and develop, through each rebirth, in an emotional and spiritual cycle as well.

If you're reading this, you might be thinking why is Aoife Ryan talking about the Celtic past if she and others are experiencing interaction with these beings today ?

In this Modern age, people don't tend to use the kind of labels that went with Otherworldly beings in the past. 'Aliens' conjures up a more modern picture.

British astronaut, Helen Patricia Sharman, went on a space mission in May of 1991 to visit the Soviet Mir space station,

She recently indicated that there could be alien beings living among us on Earth: "It's possible they're here right now and we simply can't see them."

In fact, she has added "Aliens exist, there's no two ways about it."

Could she have seen something or experienced something while in outer space that has given her a heightened sensitivity to detecting Otherworldly phenomena?

Maybe cosmic rays soaked her body and mind, producing or stoking a dormant cognitive capability that allows for sensing the presence of alien species ? Similar to how your pet dog or cat has a kind of sixth sense that we humans do not have; it could be that Helen now possesses a subliminal capability of sensing strange visions.

Admittedly, realising that there have been over 500 people that have gone into outer space, one must ask how come the other space travellers have not had the same revelation ? Come to think of it, maybe some have indeed experienced the same, but are tight-lipped else concerned that the rest of the Earth-bonded people might misperceive them as crazy or mentally unhinged. Put yourself into their shoes.

If you had never experienced encounters with supernatural beings, but suspected that there were alien creatures here on Earth, yet you had no solid proof and merely had a nagging inner feeling about it, would you speak up? On the one hand, perhaps out of loyalty to your fellow humans, you might feel it was your duty to let the unknowing know what's been/is happening. But, since there's seemingly no means to validate your claim, would you be merely ridiculed, and anyway what good would it do if humanity actually acknowledged that aliens were living here on Earth and visiting regularly, even interacting with humans.

Let's momentarily agree that there are aliens from outer space, or whatever from wherever, right here, right now, and while you are reading this sentence, they could be near you, looking over your shoulder, or possibly far away on another continent. Perhaps you, like me, know they are here, even related to some of us. If they are here and can assume human form, do you have any tangible means to ascertain that a human walking past you is a real human or instead an alien creature? Rather than taking on human form, aliens could be disguised as dogs, or cows, or trees or birds. The aliens could even be micro-organisms. As such, they are so tiny that they could be just about anywhere.

Some say that aliens are immersed in another dimension and this is one that we humans cannot see or enter into.
The British astronaut might have somehow miraculously become attached to a mini-portal into that other dimension, or there was leakage from the unseen dimension that happened while she was circling the Earth in outer space.

Maybe only some humans are open to, or susceptible to, the presence and influence of alien beings. If, as some say, they could be on Earth, but hiding, it could be that they are in plain sight and they don't believe themselves to be hiding. With that logic, we could consider that they are hiding because they have no means to show themselves to us, or they are hiding because they are waiting for something to act as a trigger for them to come out of hiding.

In my case that could be because the goddess *Aoife* lost a sister in the Otherworld and I happened to be her namesake and just the right age (12) when she needed me. Did she seek me out ? Or, was it pre-ordained ? Such a trigger might suddenly have allowed her to interact with me, which otherwise she would not been able to do, or have had no desire to do. The trigger could also be pre-ordained, so each Otherworldly beings know individually when it is finally time to interact with the Earthly partner who complements them. My Otherworldly sisters visit me. I have even flown in the sky on a broom and a horse ! I have visited the Otherworld, which has actually been a parallel version of our natural world. Not cities or towns, but forests, fields and rivers. Maybe that's because these are magical in themselves.

Remember "down the rabbit hole" which is a metaphor for the entry into the unknown. It's exactly what happens in Lewis Carroll's 'Alice in Wonderland'. The rabbit hole is the place where everything begins. It symbolises a gateway into a new world of adventures, and unknown territories. I always think that maybe Carroll used Alice, a child, because of the innocence of childhood, giving her a purity of soul. I see that as applying to me. I was only 12 years old when *Aoife* revealed herself to me.

In conclusion, I have examined the often problematic role those from the Otherworld have played both in the myths of the Celtic people and my own life. The beings and the myths are fascinating. It is easy to point the finger at males and their violent ways as reasons for the disruption of peace in the world, but of course matters are not so simple. I see some evidence of the violence of women as well. Equal status for women is important and almost always elusive in any society. Perhaps I wish we could look to the Earthly past and the Otherworld for evidence of a better time for women and the world in general. We should look for reasons as to why our world has become so violent and bloodthirsty and seek to change it.

There is intriguing evidence found in myth, literature and historical accounts. Archaeology has played an important role in finding evidence from past lives. I hope that diaries and journals like my own may also throw light up on the subject.

This poem by Irish poet, Seamus Heaney (1939 - 2013) describes the symbolic struggle that endures, and the still tragic modern study of the goddess, that is endlessly fascinating:

> "*Our mother ground*
> *is sour with blood*
> *of her faithful, who lie gargling*
> *in her sacred heart…*
> *Those who come to Ireland to 'report us fairly'*
> *must tell 'how we slaughter*
> *for the common good,…*
> *how the goddess swallows*
> *our love and terror.*"

---

(21) The Mystery of Three

Date:1969

I'm at home, sitting in the garden, listening to the birds. I have borrowed a book from *Da's* bookshelf. The book is called 'The Mystery of Three'. I remember *Aoife* telling me about three and its importance in the Otherworld.

The book tells me that there are many words which we use to express three. For example, three itself, trinity, triad, triplets, triangle, triumvirate, troika and lots more.

"The idea of the symbolic number 3 takes us on a journey, back to a remote antiquity. ..."

That sounds interesting. I like the idea of travelling back into the mists of time. I read that 3 exists in every area of knowledge known to us. 3 takes us into the realms of mythology, religion, mathematics, philosophy and magic. Wow !

It's fascinating. Apparently, as well as being an important number now, it was also so in the distant past. 3 is also recognised across the history of many diverse lands and their peoples.

When I was little, without knowing any of this, I chose 3 as my favourite number. My lucky number. Writing now, I'm not sure if this has had, or will have, any effect on my life. Could 3 have helped to shape the 'me' I am today ? I have had two best friends since I was younger. We are certainly a gaggle of 3. A disorderly trio Da calls us ! I think we prefer to think of ourselves as a 'gang'. We have had plenty of freedom. Maybe that's helped to make us more independent.

Reading on, I discover that triads and trilogies were part of the culture of ancient Greece. The gods of that time each had 3 children, for example, *Zeus* and *Hera* had 3 sons. There were 3 Cyclops and 3 Gorgons. There was also the custom of offering prayers to triads of gods. That definitely ties in with my *Aoife* and her two chosen sisters.

I think of the adventure of the Argonauts. There were 3 Argonauts who changed themselves into 3 hawks. They were successful in securing 3 of the apples of the *Hesperides*. In Greek mythology, the *Hesperides* are the nymphs of evening and golden light of sunsets, who were the 'Daughters of the Evening' or 'Nymphs of the West'. They were also called the Atlantides after their father, the royal god, *Titan Atlas*. This was in spite of the fact that the 3 daughters of the king had transformed themselves into 3 ospreys and chased them.

Later, of course, in Christian religion, 3 appeared as the Father, Son and Holy Spirit.

3 is said to be lucky. For example, I still say "third time lucky", when attempting a challenging task.

So, what started the phenomenon of 3 as a special number?

Whilst I am pondering this question, I hear a slight rustle above me. Without looking up, I know it's *Aoife*.

She hovers in her girlish persona and joins the conversation I have been having in my mind.

"If you want to think of 3 in a spiritual sense, you have to put aside thoughts of times tables and the measuring of geometric angles learnt in school. You need to free your mind from all preconceived notions about the number in terms of mathematics and open your imagination in order to enter into the mysterious notion of 3."

Instantly, I see the point she is making. I close my eyes and focus on clearing my mind.

Aoife continues. "Once you are orientated, you can begin your exploration. To borrow an expression from the human, Aristotle, "begin with matters terrestrial and transfer them to matters celestial."

I try not to concentrate too hard. To let my spirit take over.

Aoife's gentle voice floats into my brain.

"Think of 3 as in a grouping of things that are closely related or naturally connected together. A simple instance is 'father, mother, and child'. These 3 form a family as you have yourself. "

I think of God, Jesus and the Holy Spirit. They are certainly thought of as a sacred family by Catholics and other Christians.

"Tell me what you know," instructs *Aoife*.

I speak aloud. "In literature, there are plenty of examples. Alexandre Dumas' 'The Three Musketeers' immediately comes into my mind because I read that not so long ago. Then there are "the three weird sisters" in Shakespeare's 'Macbeth'. …..Oh yes, Samuel Taylor Coleridge told the tale of 'The Ancient Mariner' to 3 wedding guests. In one part it reads, "I've won! Quoth she and whistles thrice." I know this because we practised reciting it aloud in class.

Aoife nods enthusiastically. Now think of arithmetic. Did you know that the three-in-one idea was given its simplest expression in mathematics. You've heard of Pythagorus ?"

Yuk geometry ! "Yes," I answer cautiously.

"Ah, but a group called The Pythagoreans saw the triangle as far more than just a shape. They adopted the triangle and called it the most perfect geometrical figure. That's because it was the first shape to be complete in itself. It became accepted after that that the number 3 drawn as a triangle, was a perfect representation of a perfect number."

"So more like a picture that an artist might have drawn or painted ?"

"If you like," replies *Aoi*fe. "Remember, the ancient Greeks had multiple gods. The triangle was like the gods, immortal, perfect and sacred."

I consider this. It's an amazing extension of what has seemed something quite simple and uninteresting.

"To take that a step further, things in triads are the handiwork of we gods and goddesses. Think of the natural world," says *Aoife*.

Of course, *Banba* comes to mind immediately.

"Look around you." Aoife waves her arm and a ray of sunlight seems to follow in the direction she is pointing. "Natural groupings of 3s are all round. Birth, life, and death. Land, sky and water. The sun, the moon and the stars….."

I interrupt, "and the moon has 3 phases: new, full and quarter…oh, and there are the 3 dimensions of length, width and depth."

Aoife grins. It's like a game. How many examples can we think of ? " 3 states of matter: solid, liquid and gases. The categories of 3 as in animal, vegetable and mineral….

I jump in again. "Even human bodies include 3s.
The 3 main parts of the body are the head, the trunk and the limbs."

Aoife's too quick for me. "and your facial parts, eyes, nose mouth. "

"Fingers and legs both have 3 sections," I add.

We stop and both laugh together.

"So you see," explains *Aoife*, "It is only natural that your Earthly world is divided into earth, sky and water. For True Earthly Believers, like yourself, there is also the threefold division of the Cosmos into Earth, Sky and the Otherworld."

I love to learn in this way. No tutting nuns and dry text books. This is real education.

"So you can see," continues my mentor, "although the concept of 3 is an abstract, you can apply it to things in both a practical sense and a spiritual one. Number 3 is especially sacred to True Believers. Otherwordly beings are portrayed by you in groups of 3. We symbolise fire, breath and water and the earth, sky and sea. Operating within these threefold cosmologies, forms a frame for our unified identity."

I want to ask questions, but *Aoife* puts a finger to her lips. "I must depart sister. I know you are one who has been given the honour of service to your fellows in this world and beyond. That time is the future to come. You are at the start. Be rich in love, yet always humble. Remember, a soul and spirit begin in the heart and are honestly won. Simply be for now, a girl with a pure heart and soul. That's what you are. That's what this world…." *Aoife* sighs. "and mine, need."

Rather as if a magician had waved a wand, *Aoife* vanishes and is gone, just a twinkling mist remains which soon dissipates into the air.

I muse for a moment on our exchange. Then return to my book. I read that The *Morrígan* is interesting in terms of 'threeness'. She is described as a trio of sisters, named "the three Morrígna". The sisters' names vary in different versions of the story, but ones frequently given are *Badb, Macha and Nemain*. Of course, *Macha* is a very familiar name.

The three Morrígna are believed to be sisters of the three land goddesses *Ériu, Banba* and *Fódla*. *Banba*, another sister of mine ! The Morrígan herself is married to the god, *Dagda* (Da) and is a shape-shifting goddess. Her two sisters are said to be the wives of *Neit,* a god of war.

The Morrigan trio is associated with the banshee of later Irish folklore.

The *Morrígan*'s modern Gaelic name is *Mór-Ríoghain* which has been translated as 'great queen' or 'phantom queen'. She is mainly associated with war and fate, especially with foretelling doom, death or victory in battle. In this role she often appears as a *badb* (crow) She incites warriors to battle and can help bring about victory over their enemies. The *Morrígan* encourages warriors to do brave deeds, to strike fear into their enemies. Yet, on the maternal side, she is portrayed washing the bloodstained clothes of those fated to die. The dual-nature again. She has also been seen as a manifestation of the Earth, a sovereignty-goddess, representing the goddess' role as a guardian of an area of land and its people.

In what the book calls Celtic 'symbology', numbers play an important role. They are thought of as whole concepts, not just simple mathematical numbers. Every number has a particular, special character of its own. Three-headed Celtic gods and goddesses are incorporated into threes. For example, The *Dagda*, the father-god of the earth and ruler over life and death, had three daughters, known as the three *Brigits* (my Auntie's, Mam's sister's name. Each one of these had a particular skill and the three combined were seen as a symbol of fertility and life. *Brigit* is also associated with serpents, an ancient symbol of the healing powers of the Earth Goddess. Their festival is at Imbolc (St. Brigit's day) at the start of February to mark the Celtic start of Spring. She is the goddess of 3 qualities, independence, integrity and energy. She is often depicted in her threefold aspect with fiery red hair or fair hair like *Aoife*. This colouring is a common aspect of both Celtic women and goddesses. Symbols and things associated with the *Brigits* are fire, wells for water, healing cauldrons, serpents, anvils and hammers, dandelions, amethysts and white candles.

Words related to 3, are also found in the Celtic 'treskele' or 'tripal' spiral. This is composed of 3 pulsating and swirling spirals which are forever in motion. These were said to signify the three-layered nature of the human soul, namely, active, passive and neutral.

Spirals cover the entrances of all pre-historic standing stones and entrances to caverns and caves. This three-fold symmetry of megalithic architecture is so ancient its origins disappear into the mists of time. Nevertheless, as the books tells me, we know that it relates to the 3 elements of life, death and prophecy (future).

'Dolmens' are a type of single-chamber megalithic tomb, usually consisting of two or more vertical megaliths supporting a large flat horizontal capstone, like the shape of a huge table. Most date from the early Neolithic period. They were often covered with earth or smaller stones to form a 'tumulus': a mound of earth and stones raised over a grave/s. Important artefacts related to the triple symbolism has been found in many areas occupied by ancient Celtic peoples. Many carved stones outside entrances to these mounds are inscribed with triad spirals intertwining with one another, symbolising unity and evolution. It's so fascinating.

Three can also be found in other societies. It represents the Hindu trinities of *Brahma, Vishnu* and *Shiva.* Three can be seen on ornaments and architecture of all Hindu cultures. This links to the three-headed Celtic gods and goddesses. Celtic works of art are grouped in threes: strange creatures with 3 heads, one head with 3 faces, or one body with 3 heads.

In ancient times, male heroes often travelled on their journeys in threes. There is a belief that 'the triad' means 'the seen' and the 'unseen' with a third indicating 'mystery' in between.

'C' is the third letter of the alphabet and the beginning of the word 'Celt' and the first letter of the Celtic words *cén fàth, cén ait, cén chaoi* (why, where, when).

One of the most well-known emblems of Ireland, the three leafed shamrock. We learnt at school that it is also a Celtic metaphor which represents the Holy Trinity and what it means to us on Earth: to hold trust in your soul, belief in your heart and faith in your mind.

Legend has it that St. Patrick, who brought Christianity to Ireland, once plucked a three-leafed clover, (*shamrog* / shamrock, to illustrate the doctrine of the Holy Trinity, Father, Son and Holy Spirit. The three leaves of a shamrock are seen as standing for faith, hope and love. A fourth leaf is where we get the luck from. The four-leafed clover is uncommon and is just a variation of the three-leafed clover. All Irish people consider it to be a symbol of good luck.

Over centuries, Celtic Spirituality spread right across all the territories where the Celtic people live. Right across from the East to the whole of Gaul (Europe) as well as Ireland and Britain. This spirituality still exists worldwide. Traditions and links with spirituality have been handed down through the ages. Da explained to me that belief in spirituality means no separation between the natural world and the life of spirit, It is an ongoing, holistic (new word for me), view of the world. All science, spirituality, nature, religion, and the Otherworld as one, not separate.

Aoife has mentioned on several occasions, that this inclusive view means being ready to open up my horizons to encompass a spiritual, as well as a physical, existence.

"This, in turn," she explained, "will enable you to see a world beyond your own imagination."

She followed on, "remember, Three is also a symbol of the Triple Goddess , a maiden like you represents youth, your Mam represents mother and maturity. Old age is represented by a crone. Long in the future for you." She smiled "Each of these symbolises both a separate stage in your Earthly female life cycle and the three phases of the moon: new, half and full."

'Threeness' or 'triad', has always been considered sacred in the Catholic Church. For myself and my family, Three is also a representation of ideas and energies that come to us from the Otherworld in a magical and mysterious manner.
The threesome is a symbol of the unity of body, mind and spirit. It can be spirit, mind and body in a circle of synthesis or past, present and future enclosed in the ring of eternity and also, art, science and religion bound together in a circle making up our culture.

I pause and my eyes close. I feel content. I close my eyes and I feel, rather than see, the presence of my sister, my guardian, *Aoife*.

She whispers in my ear. "I am pleased you are happy, young Earthly sister. Happiness, like a flower, is a quiet blooming of the soul. You are opening your eyes and loving the world around you. You are at peace, at one, with your surroundings and your connection to the natural world. Lie back and let the happiness soak right into your bones."

I close my eyes and savour the moment, slowly releasing my soul towards sleep. I lie back in my chair. My body and mind relax. The garden is alive with a compendium of birds. Their song is told through their rich emotional intelligence. For those capable of real listening, the message is clear. In that moment, my mind becomes clear. There are no expectations lying heavy on my conscience. No deadlines for homework. No schedules to meet for household tasks. I feel as if I have made it. I am a winner. I hear and understand the tune of the natural world. I close my eyes and let the song enter my heart. I feel *Aoife* blowing me a kiss. Sleep creeps over me. I drift into the world of dreams.

---

(22) Da and Druids

Date: 1969

Da and I are sitting in his study. He's been explaining to me about how it can be difficult to be a Druid, or pagan, parent in a Catholic society.

He begins with a question. "What does it mean to be both a Catholic and a Druid?"

"Is it even possible to be both?" I ask. "I have wondered."

"Well, I'm sure you realise that both have several key areas where they are in agreement. For instance, a respect for learning, revering tradition and perhaps most important for us True Believers, a regard for the beauty of the natural world."

Your Gran and Granda wanted me to follow in their footsteps, but they didn't want to force anything. It was them, of course, who sparked my interest in Druidry to begin with."

I'm pleased to hear this.

"Nevertheless, there are conflicts which I am still trying to clarify for myself."

I settle back to hear the story.

Da takes a puff on his pipe. "The Druids of the ancient world were contemporaries of the Romans. If you think of the oral tradition in stories of gods and goddesses, we know much that was written in medieval times was by Christian monks who inevitably were biased against a culture of multiple deities. It's the same with ancient Druids. What we know about them was written by the Romans. They weren't originally Christian at that time, but they worshipped the old gods of Rome. They saw the Druids as a problem and made it their objective to destroy them. They destroyed the sacred places and oak groves. For example, at Anglesey in Wales in about AD 63. The Roman destruction of the Druids was really based on politics rather than religion, because the Druids were the power behind the indigenous Celtic resistance to Roman occupation of Celtic lands, and imperial Rome did not like freedom fighters !"

"Like Queen Boudicca of the Iceni tribe ?" I've been reading about her.

"That's it.'

"We also know that St. Patrick had gigantic political and spiritual conflicts with the Druids of his time, several centuries later. Remember that the Druids of England and Wales had long since disappeared under the Romans and the widespread religious path turned to Christianity. Whereas here, in Ireland, the Druids were and have been, the real keepers of the traditional ways of the old Irish and Celtic cultures. Unfortunately, the differences of the Druids and Christians, are fundamental and even now, in many ways, irreconcilable."

It's a shame," I remark.

"The old cultures, both Celtic and Roman Catholic, didn't separate religion from politics, and that was also a part of the problem. St. Patrick didn't destroy the oak tree groves as the Romans did, but he destroyed images of Celtic gods, as at *Magh-Slecht*, where he is said to have destroyed the idol *Crom-Cruach*, to which human sacrifice was said to have taken place."

"So there isn't proof of human sacrifice there ?"

"No, but St. Patrick must have known that it would be something which Christians would find unacceptable." He pauses while we both consider the implications. Then Da continues.

"So with the conversion to Catholicism of the Irish under St. Patrick, and the destruction of Druidry by the Romans in the rest of the Celtic world, the old 'paleodruids', as we know them, had disappeared from history by about 500 AD. With the Roman conquest of Gaul the fact is that the Druids lost all their jurisdiction. They suffered a great decline in status and there is no reason to believe that not much power, that the ancient Druids had, survived after about 77AD. That's the date of the last mention of the Druids as still even being in existence.

"So how did the Druids recover themselves ?"

Well, obviously, there would have been small numbers scattered here and there throughout Gaul (Europe). Many Druids escaped to Britain. The Emperors Tiberius and Claudius abolished certain practices in the cult of the Druids, such as their organization, and their assemblies. We have to remember that it didn't take place overnight. The disappearance was gradual."

There's a lot for me to think about here.

"The modern view is that the Romans were afraid of the Druids because they were teachers of the Gallo-Roman youth and judges at trials. They had power in this respect. The pre-Christian Romans were very superstitious. For them, the Druids of Gaul, Britain and Ireland were seen as magicians, diviners and physicians. If you think of the saga tales of Ireland, they're most often found in the service of kings, who employed them as advisers because of their powers in magic. Like all good magicians, they had wands…."

I interrupt with a giggle.

Da smiles. "In the exercise of these powers, the Druids made use of wands, made from yew trees. They wrote in a secret language called *Ogham*. This was called their "keys of wisdom."

"Tell me more about *Ogham*. I've never heard of it."

"It's very interesting, " Da tells me. "Ogham was an Early Medieval alphabet used mainly to write down the early Irish language. You can still see the language on stone inscriptions. Between about the 4th to 6th centuries AD, it was called the 'orthodox' language. Later, over the 6th to 9th centuries, the old Irish language was what became known as 'scholastic ogham'. The vast majority of the inscriptions consist of personal names, like a cemetery stone."

"Are there any round here ?"

"Yes. Munster has the largest number of inscriptions in Ireland. We'll go to look soon, OK ?"

I nod.

"What's interesting in terms of the natural world, is that according to the records, the names of various trees can be ascribed to individual letters. The etymology of the word *ogham* remains unclear. It's a shame because in the study of the origin of words and the way their meanings have changed throughout history, it's often possible to trace them back. One possible origin is from the Irish *og-úaim* 'which means 'point-seam', referring to the seam that's made by the point of a sharp weapon."

"Or wand ?" I suggest. "Like a sword."

"Anything's possible," agrees Da. "That's the fun of investigating it."

Mam arrives with cups of tea and a pile of biscuits. She smiles at us, then speaks to Da. "Don't give her a headache with all that information, Dagda."

"No, I love it," I exclaim, spraying crumbs from the biscuit I'm munching into the air.

Mam leaves us to it. I can hear that she's put on a record to listen to. I listen to the dulcet tones of the tenor, John McCormack. I know he was celebrated for his performances of both operatic and popular song. Mam told me he was renowned for his diction and breath control. He was made a Papal Count by Pope Pious XI for his donations to Catholic charities.

John McCormack, tenor (1884-1945)

It's an old '78' record that Mam's listening to and is a bit scratched, but his voice still sounds lovely. It's Mam's favourite song called 'The Star of the County Down'. It's a romantic song about a young man falling in love with a beautiful maiden. A kind of fairy tale.

Da and I finish our tea.

"Do you want me to go on ?" he enquires.

"Of course." I am soaking up this information like a sponge and I hope it will stay in my memory for ever.

"I mentioned that in Ireland and Gaul, the ancient Druids enjoyed a high reputation for learning, and some Irish Druids even held a rank higher than that of the king."

So, unfortunately, as far as the ancient Druids go, we know little about what they believed from their own perspective. They left no writings and they were gone from history by 500 AD in Ireland."

"So, all the conflicts they had with the Romans were because of their political power in terms of Celtic identity and resistance against Roman rule over Celtic lands ?"

"That's it in a nutshell. And, remember, all the persecution was essentially political at the start, even before the Romans began to adopt Christianity. The real religious battles in Ireland started when St. Patrick began his mission. Patrick was also an emissary of Rome because, at that time, Rome saw religion and politics inextricably linked together."

St. Patrick himself was fighting on behalf of the Church against what he saw as idolatry, superstition, and magic. He was really the vanguard for the Roman Empire. It was the start a major and widespread cultural change, both political and religious. We might say, the ancient Druids saw the writing on the wall, and they were determined to fight to protect their way of life from the coming of inevitable changes."

"M'mm," I ponder.

"I think Mam's right. Let knock things on the head for now and continue another time."

"OK," I agree reluctantly.

(23) Crystals from the Otherworld

Date:1968

Healing in The Otherworld is very different from medicine or use of doctors on Earth. Many religions base the healing process on on the powers of different herbs and crystals. These methods date back to infinity and are important to both True Believers and Druids.

Crystal healing here on Earth is seen as an alternative medical practice that uses semi-precious stones and crystals such as quartz, agate, amethyst or opals. Many medical practitioners here regard it all as phoney or pseudo-science, but they have closed minds.

Both Mam and *Aoife* have educated me about the use of crystals. Aoife told me what powers each crystal had and Mam encouraged me to use them as protectors against illness and disease, as well as having negative, angry thoughts.

Mam had said that I should have favourite or special crystals and carry them in a little bag in my pocket or round my neck. I can't hang them round my neck at school because they would count as jewellery, which is not allowed, well, other than crucifixes or holy medallions to Our Lady or possibly St. Christopher, who keeps travellers safe.

Aoife added that I should sleep with my special crystal / s under my pillow. Mam knows that crystals often get lost or misplaced by children, so she keeps a few extras on hand.

This is what I have learnt about crystals. I am recording the information in my journal to remind me.

Aoife explained much to me over a series of visits.

On the first occasion, I was sitting in my bedroom doing my homework. I sensed the air change. I knew what was happening.

From the twilight, a yawn wafts into my ears. I gaze across the room, in anticipation. From a distant star travelling through the twinkle of eternity is an owl. It flys through my window and perches on the dressing table. I'm not afraid. I know this is *Aoife* in another guise, a great and wise bird. I hold my breath.

***Aoife* as the owl.**

Before I can breathe again, before my brain was capable of any other notion, I found myself, my being, behind those green owl eyes. Now, I am the one in the sky looking down at the ground far below. A real bird's eye view ! I know that these eyes are those which watch all the galaxies in the dominion of love. The ones that belong to my guardian, my goddess. To her, me, the child Aoife, her little sister, is a speck on the Earth.

My own eyes return to my room, safe and happy at home. The owl's eyes returned to their owner who continues to watch me closely from her perch. At the same moment, I am aware that there in the sky, there in a place that touches our reality, links with it and yet belongs to another.

I study the owl as she settles. She is very pretty and statuesque. She has distinctive ear tufts. The upper parts of the tufts are mottled with deep, night sky colouring mixed with tawny brown. Her wings and tail are barred in colour and light . Her underside is varying shades of hued buff, again streaked with a deep, dark colouring. Her face merges into her head. It's a soft shade of white and cream. Her orange eyes are most distinctive and I guess all-seeing I estimate she is almost thirty inches in height and her wingspan could be more than four feet. From the brown-flecked duskiness of her plumage she seems mature, but not old.

The owl speaks. "I see you have an Amethyst, young sister."

I have it on a chain around my neck and I touch it self-consciously. "It's my favourite crystal," I tell her shyly.

"A wise choice my child. "The first and most important of crystals is the Amethyst. It's known as a "Master Healing Crystal". "

The owl stretches a wing as if to touch the stone. "An Amethyst's most notable healing quality is its ability to purify and transmute all forms of negativity. Did you know that ?"

"Mam did tell me that. She encourages me to be positive and calm."

The owl nods approval. "For children like yourself who are in transition...that means growing, but not yet fully mature, a major disappointment can be made not to feel so you're your Amethyst can absorb all negative emotions and provide you with comfort through spiritual acceptance."

I must look puzzled because she explains, "you accept help from the stone through your heart, not your mind. It's your soul which is being comforted."

I think I understand.

"When you feel pain, having an Amethyst close to you will help clear unwanted discharged energies. For example, if you are sad or feeling negative about something whilst you are in this bedroom, stroking the Amethyst will bring the room back into a balanced state. If you are in pain, hold the Amethyst directly on or over the area of the pain. Depending on how bad the pain is, this can take up to 20 minutes. "

"Thank you, *Aoife*...wise owl..."

"Would you like to hear about more stones ?"

"Yes please."

"Have you heard of an "Apache Tear" ?

I shake my head.

"It's also called the "Grief Stone".

Apache Tear is actually 'Obsidian'. "

"What's that ?"

"It's a natural glass which is formed by the cooling of molten lava from a volcano. It's very dark in colour, but transparent. When you hold a small piece up to the light you can see through it. If you use an Apache Tear to absorb any negative emotions, you will see it cloud up and become opaque. You won't be able to see through it. It will usually become clear again after the sad time is over."

While *Aoife* has been talking, I have got out my little notebook where I write down things I don't want to forget. I write down the name 'Apache Tear'.

Aoife waits patiently while I write down the name. She then adds a warning. "Remember though that obsidian can be dangerous when you handle it. If you break it into pieces, the curved surfaces of the pieces are razor thin and extremely sharp. Over time, ancient peoples learned to break obsidian to make tools."

Another stone which is useful is 'Aventurine'. It's known as the "Leadership Stone". It strengthens and restores the energy of your heart. It provides a person with a balance of energies. This crystal is green. It protects the heart and is very loving, embracing the Heart. Children who are shy or timid and afraid to show their leadership qualities need a crystal like Aventurine. " She looks at me and smiles. "I don't think you have such a problem, young Aoife !"

I laugh.

"It does help you to become and remain active though. It helps you to use your initiative."

That's what both Mam and Da tell me. I make a mental note that it would be good to acquire an Aventurine.

"Let's see. Ah yes, there is the Carnelian. It's a Self-Esteem Crystal. It helps to restore feelings of inadequacy and low self-esteem. "

"You mean not believing in yourself or thinking you can't do something ?"

"That's it." She smiles approvingly. I think it's a smile. It's hard to tell with a bird's beak, but it rises up and down.

"The deep orange colours of this stone relate to strengthening and promoting self-security and self-love. Believing in yourself. The pinker shades relate to enhancing love between a child and its parent, through self-acceptance."

"Like if I accept myself as me, they accept me for what I am ?"

"Something like that. The Carnelian is also used to help with skin conditions, like spots or acne. You hold the stone over the area of skin affected and move it in circles for several minutes, several times a day."

I hope I never get teenage acne, but I've made a note just in case. I do have a friend with the problem. I wonder if she knows about the Carnelian.

"Then there are two different types of Quartz. They are they the 'Clear' and the 'Rose'. Clear Quartz is known as "The Healing Crystal". It's a general all-purpose healing crystal. In a cluster, each one has its own energy and a healing mission. If a child makes contact with the right crystal, the energy is discharged either very slowly, or quite suddenly, sothat it feels like a very mild electric shock !"

"I don't like the sound of that !"

The owl tips her head to one side, as if curious or surprised at my response. "Ah, but such natural energy can be just enough to transform a disharmonious thought pattern, maybe burn off some negative emotional state, or even place the spiritual seeds of a child's future into consciousness. Using a cluster of Clear Quartz crystals for children is particularly nice. Many individuals in a cluster act in different ways. There's a crystal for any occasion! Crystal clusters are also helpful to organize scattered thoughts and to deflect negative energies."

"What about the Rose Quartz ?" I ask.

It's called "The Love Stone". It's another very important general healing crystal for children. If a child has a lot of hurt feelings or aggressive tendencies. Rose Quartz can soothe a broken heart. It helps a child to understand that sometimes we have to accept the ways things are, rather than the way we'd like them to be. A Rose Quartz can sooth all kinds of erratic emotional states, anxiety, fear, compulsions, and even more serious mental disorders. Sometimes the brain can benefit if the Rose Quartz is guided over the nerve centres. It makes muscles relax. For young hearts, Rose Quartz helps to keep the Heart 'chakra' open, keep it vital and protected, filtering in the good energies and keeping out the bad ones."

I remember that Da told me about chakra. It's various focal points which are used in a variety of meditation practices .It helps with breathing. It's to do with the sense of psychic energy centres.

"I'm sure you know of Lapis Lazuli ," says the owl. "It's known as a "Psychic Balance Stone". Lapis Lazuli is an incredible stabiliser for children who show psychic gifts early in life. The deep blue colour stimulates the expansion of consciousness in a helpful way. The crystal promotes purification and clarity of spiritual insight. Lapis Lazuli provides self-acceptance of your individual given gifts. It encourages openness of one's spiritual awareness. This stone is highly prized for its protective powers and stimulation of all psychic senses."

This is a crystal I love. I have a piece Lapis lazuli, or lapis for short. I read that as well as being an intense shade of blue, it's a metamorphic rock. Ancients prized it as semi-precious. This is a treasure to me. I have held it in my hands, pressed against my body as I sleep. It is wonderful.

"Another stone is Jade which is an ornamental mineral, mostly known for its amazing varieties of the colour green. It can also appear in other colours as well, mainly yellow and white."

"Jade is often used in jewellery," I remark.

"It's also a "Soother of Emotions Stone", the owl informs me. Jade is easily obtained and can be worn as jewellery, as you say. Emotionally sensitive children often need a supportive system to ensure that their feelings don't overwhelm them. Jade is good for enhancing confidence, self-assurance, and self-reliance. It's inspirational in helping you to achieve your desires in life."

"Mam has a beautiful ring with a jade stone set in it. Da bought it for their wedding anniversary.

"Tiger Eye is another," states the owl. It's a "Grounding Stone" When you rock it back and forth the light reflects in a certain way as if the tiger's eye were winking at you ! "

I immediately decide I must seek one out.

This stone is excellent for grounding your psychic energy and providing security for opening up the psychic centres. Sometimes, I know, like other children, you can get carried away and get lost in your dream world."

This is true of me.

"Tiger Eye helps to pull you back into your body. That's important if you have been engaging in astral travel. This stone is very useful to put action into your thoughts. Tiger's Eye is all about being practical !"

I am still scribbling in my note book. *Aoife* waits patiently.

"The last one I shall mention to you is Pyrite. It's a "Protection Stone."

"I know this one. I've learnt about it in school," I tell *Aoife* excitedly. "The mineral pyrite, or iron pyrite, is also known as fool's gold. Gold prospectors sometimes thought it was gold. It's an iron sulfide with the chemical formula FeS_2. Pyrite is the most abundant sulfide mineral. Pyrite has a metallic lustre and a pale brass-yellow hue which gives it a superficial resemblance to gold." I stop, realising I'm showing off.

"You're right, says the owl. "Iron Pyrite comes in many different shapes, from sun discs to cubes. Children are attracted to its shiny brassy surfaces. Pyrite is like a small mirror through which negative energy can be reflected away. The fear of being unprotected is reduced. There is also a feeling of physical empowerment, that life in the physical form is perfect, and love is abundant."

What a lovely finish to the story, I think.

Dusk had fallen, bringing moonlight.. *Aoife* as the owl ruffles her feathers. She rises majestically her huge wings opening. Pointing at the window, she melts into the wall and disappears through the closed window.

(24) A Wolf Story

"We don't learn about trees without climbing and sleeping in them. We can't understand caves without spending time in them alone in the dark. We won't appreciate the wildness of wolves without hearing them howl in the night…"

(Belden C. Lane in 'The Great Conversation')

Date 1967

I am asleep. I awake to the sound of a wolf's cry. *Faoladh*, I think immediately. Sure enough, I open my eyes and look around. *Faoladh* is nearby, but I don't recognise the surroundings.

Close by, moving in the early morning light is a wolf. She is a whiteish shade of silver. Her fur is glossy and thick. She moves so gracefully. Her paws kiss the earth with such a lightness of touch that she seems to be floating above the ground.

For a moment her head turns in my direction. There is serenity in her gaze. I stand still. If she is indeed a wild wolf, I know that if I move she will take flight into the trees. I breathe slowly letting time slow down as *Aoife* has shown me. In my mind I take photographs using my eyes as a natural lens. Perhaps in this time bubble, I will dream of being as free as she, out here with nature, living with her family. I watch as she continues her journey and is gone beyond the horizon.

Faoladh approaches me. "Welcome to wolf territory, Aoife."

He is in the form of a wolf today. As beautiful and elegant as the wolf I have just seen. I look at him enquiringly.

"I wish to show you the home of the wolves. Sadly, on Earth, we are gone from your land of Ireland."

"Where are we now ?"

"Just say, it's wolf country."

I feel a sense of guilt, even though it's not my fault. Why do people traditionally think of wolves as bad and evil ? I can't help thinking of the story of 'Little Red Riding Hood' and the Big Bad Wolf who tricked her. But, *Faoladh* has always taken care of me and is good.

Faoladh reads my mind. "I will show you the best side of wolves, their families, their habitats….Come."

He raises a paw and turns, heading into a forest. I follow, trusting him completely.

As we enter a clearing in the trees, *Faoladh* points to the crest of a hill. I can see several wolfish silhouettes. Two of them are standing almost statue-like while others tumble about, playing, pulling one another over. When the Alpha wolf howls, they all stop instantly, like children obeying the teacher's whistle.

Faoladh points out that the youngsters have been invited to a family feast. They join the adults. Together, the wolves fill the still air with their singing. I imagine that they are singing a wolf hymn, a song without words as humans know them, but just the sound, the language, of pure joy in nature and their home territory.

These wolves are nothing like the monsters of fairy tales. I'm sure they sense I am here, but instead of being aggressive they appear docile, even shy. *Faoladh* encourages me to approach the group. They know him. He is one of them, but what about me ?

A young female, not fully grown, comes warily towards me. I don't know who is most nervous me or her ! To my amazement, she rolls onto her back with her tail wagging like a family dog. As we draw closer, I can see that her body bears scars. I reach out a hand, as I would for a dog who didn't know me, so she can learn my scent first. All the time watching me with those ever alert eyes, she sniffs my hand. Before I can respond, she springs up on hind legs, pushing her weight against me.

Faoladh smiles. He knows this member of his family does not want to threaten me, even though I'm a human stranger. Neither of us are a threat to one another. She just wants to be friends. A wild creature and a human child, each recognising that we are kindred spirits.

"Her name is *Luna*, after the moon," explains *Faoladh* .

She is warm and soft to the touch. I notice it is daytime now. *Luna* lies down at my feet. I stand still, unable to take my eyes off this amazing creature. Here in the sunshine, my eyes close. It feels blissful. Just listening to the music of the skies and the song of the wolves, moving to the rhythm. There is something so right about being there together. I feel as if nature craved my presence at this joyful moment. I lie down next to *Luna* and together we enjoy the rays of the sun on our faces.

After a while, I feel a gentle touch on my shoulder. It's *Faoladh*. "Shall we move on?" he suggests.

I am reluctant to move, but *Luna* stirs, rises up on her four paws. We make eye contact. Then she is gone.

"You see the lesson you have learned here ?" asks *Faoladh*.

I nod lazily and happily. I am still back with *Luna.* I force my mind into listening mode.

"Lessons in classrooms can only tell a limited part of the whole story. Only by engaging yourself with all the elements , wind and fire, earth and tree, the song of the birds and the cry of the wolf, will you ever be able to understand the language of nature whispered through it all. You must listen all the time. Make contact, as you have today with *Luna*. Never stop. Give your heart and soul to the wild things in the world."

I nod agreement. This experience has made things clearer.

"You see," continues my wolf friend, "everything is interrelated. Your Earthly reality. The reality of the Otherworld. It is all part of a united whole."

"I see. All creatures are one, despite their breed or appearance. Look at you. You can turn from a wolf to a boy, but you are still *Faoladh,* my friend."

He smiles and gently touches my cheek. "You are learning Earth child. Listen and love. Understanding will follow in time. There is no hurry."

I remember *Bile,* the old oak tree in The Woodland, told me that nature is like a spider's web, all connected, brought to life and fed by the sap of the tree of wisdom.

As we move on, the red sun is lowering in the sky, moving towards the place where it sets in the West. At the same time, a similar coloured moon is rising behind us in the East. I have seen this before and I know it's a phenomenon that happens on the night of a full moon. *Aoife* has told me that this is the time that the universe falls into what she called, "a harmonic alignment."

As we continue, we are encircled by the shadows of the wolves moving amongst the dark trees. They stay with us, hidden like a ghostly presence to watch over us.

I stir and find myself back in my bedroom. I think through my experience with the wolves. I feel privileged to have been part of the world and to have been a part of their group on their territory. When I knew they were there watching us. Invisible, yet, to me, knowing there was a watchful presence travelling through the trees. I want to hold those images, of Luna playing with me for ever.

There's still a lot I need to learn from *Faoladh* and my Otherworldly sisters. I need to treasure this memory. Lock it firmly into my mind. I know I have seen and heard the wolves, but there is still much to understand. *Aoife* would say you can't force understanding. It comes gently and some things remain 'unknowable'. The great mysteries are often beyond our Earthly seeing and knowing. That is not a fault or a problem. We have to accept some things as they are and as they seem. We can't always express in language what is in our soul. Aoife reminds me we should be humble in the 'Multiverse'. We are only a tiny part of what exists. "Humans mustn't think that everything should revolve around them."

"There is a goddess called *Loba*," *Faoladh* told me, "who preserves what's at risk of being lost on Earth In some of your countries, wolves are killed in large numbers. This is bad for the balance and harmony of the Multiverse. Loba gathers the bones of wolves which are strewn across these lands. She uses the wolf song and her singing brings them back to life again."

He also told me that wolves are associated with the night. Like me," he explained, "they are guardians, both of children and of the night. Your life span. We guide souls from Earth into their afterlife; their rebirth."

.

(25) True Believers as Parents

Date: 1969

Da and I are discussing Druidry.

"Let's start with the Sacred Rite of Naming and Welcoming a Child," suggests Da.

When we knew you were on your way, we were so thrilled and excited !"

I feel proud.

"I'm sure you don't remember the Rite of Welcome as you were only a few months old at the time !"

I grin and shake my head.

"Well, as you know, it's performed for a baby during the first year of his or her life. We thought it was better to carry out the rite while you were tiny because people have done it when the child is beginning to toddle and that can cause trouble !!"

" I can imagine," I laugh.

Anyway, Mam and I thought it would be nicer to have the ritual when you were still young enough to hold in our arms. The important thing was that us as parents, our family members and the community could feel secure that you were acknowledged and blessed as soon as possible."

It sounds silly, but I wish I did have a memory of the occasion, but I'm sure it's there, safely stored in my mind.

"It doesn't matter where the rite takes place, so we chose our garden. Other people might choose ancient sites, stone circles or standing stones, as they feel it would allow them a clear connection with distant ancestors and our heritage. We felt the garden was a personal, natural environment which was sacred for us."

I love our garden. I'm sure that's why I feel such an affinity with it. "I'm pleased you made that choice," I tell Da.

"We stood in a circle and prayers of blessing to cleanse and consecrate the area were recited. The spirits of Place must be honoured. It had to be special.

Everyone, including us, felt the spirits would approve and they would endow the garden with their spiritual energy and sense of harmony.

We also created a smaller sacred Circle wrapped in hessian and decorated with acorns, pine cones, dried oak leaves and cinnamon sticks." Da grins at me.

My personal sacred circle

I know because it sits pride of place in my bedroom and the decorations represent the time of year of my birth – November. Acorns and pine cones can be used for healing. Cinnamon is lucky and believed to help muscle pain. Oak leaves remind me of *Bile,* the Tree of Life and Wisdom.

Da has told me about the event before, but I love to hear it again. Now I'm older, I understand the rites of the ceremony better.

"Grandpa Ryan oversaw the rite, together with us and you as the child to be blessed. Your Aunt Brigid and Uncle John were named as guardians."

"Like god-parents ?"

"That's it."

Brigid is Mam's sister and John is Da's brother.

"What about the Ceremony ?"

"The ceremony itself was wholly flexible, adapting it to what we wanted. Everyone gathered around the Circle. Mam and I, me holding you, stood at the edge. The priestess bid everyone welcome. She called to the Spirits of Place that the rite may be done with their guidance and inspiration. She then makes the Call for Peace:

> *Let there be peace in the East, so let it be.*
> *Let there be peace in the South, so let it be.*
> *Let there be peace in the West, so let it be.*
> *Let there be peace in the North, so let it be.*
> *Let there be peace through all the Worlds.*
> *So let it be."*

I'm pleased it was a female priestess.

Da continues. "The priestess said something on the lines of, 'we gather here in peace for this joyful and sacred occasion that is the First Rite of Passage on the journey each of us make upon this Earth. As our Circle is woven and consecrated, this moment in time and this place becomes blessed. Let each soul truly be here that the spirits of those gathered may be blended in one sacred space, with one purpose and one voice.' "

"That's sounds lovely."

Da nods agreement. "Then the Circle was consecrated by the priestess. She called to the spirits of the Three Worlds, that the rite be blessed by the powers of all Creation."

"Tell me what she said."

Da considers. "Hail spirits of this sacred land, you whose beauty and power inspires us, as you have inspired those who came before us. Spirits of the high skies that guide us to stretch and grow. Gentle lord of the sun, distant stars and ancestral light, as well as cloud folk who paint such works of art above us, breath of life, soft breeze and chasing winds; feathered folk who know the dance of freedom upon the wing. Spirits of the dark earth that hold and feed us; mud of our lands, rich and fertile soil into which we so deeply root, rocks and stones, gems of the earth, you who give us stability underfoot; trees and plants, creatures both four footed and two."

"Wow !"

Da smiles and carries on. "Spirits of the open seas that wash and shape the shores of these lands, meandering rivers, guiding our direction, birthing springs of new life, deep still pools holding us upon our journey.

You of the tidal waters, emerging and receding, blood and rain, swimming, diving. You who offer us freedom, nourishment and rebirth. As our ancestors knew and honoured your power, so do we now. Honour this our rite, we ask you. Inspire and bless those gathered. Blessed be as blessed is."

Da pauses and we both contemplate on the words which welcomed me into this world.

"Then, the priestess made offerings to the Spirits of Place. She welcomes the three of us into the Circle. We also gave offerings to the Spirits of Place. The purpose of the rite is then declared. The priestess explained that we were gathered on that day and mentioned the phase of the moon and the year, 1953.

We were there in the eye of the Sun, upon the hallowed Earth. We were all there to witness the sacred Rite that was the Naming and Welcoming of our child, Aoife....You !"

Da and I hug one another and laugh happily together.

"We also gave thanks for the wonder of new life and recognised the honour of parenthood. We thanked you, our baby for entering our community."

I feel tearful, in a happy way though.

"We also thanked our gods and the gods of our ancestors and those who shared with us their lives, their wisdom and their love. Blessings were bequeathed to you by your ancestors of blood and spirit. We recognised that we are connected through the spirits dancing inside us, creating our lives and the worlds within which we live. We celebrated every soul being a part of the web of life. As you entered the world, you created a new seam in our family and our community."

The priestess acknowledged the enormous changes which the arrival of a child into our lives would mean.

Then she said, "Dagda and Macha over the years of your relationship, you have explored and expressed your love together, questing inspiration and sharing your creativity. Now there is another soul whose energy plays around you, creating new and exquisite patterns. Sometimes, she may tangle the threads.........."

We both grin.

Then we held hands and looked closely at one another to seal the bond between the three of us.

The priestess reminded us that things will change. Mam and I would discover new facets, new strengths, skills and depths of courage. There would be love and tenderness. As a family we would grow stronger and richer in spirit. Then we made our personal vows to each other. We had to take the principal responsibility for your mental and physical, throughout the journey of your childhood. We then gifted you the circle we had made.

The guardians had to then step forward from the edge of the Circle and agree their role as guardians.

You were then blessed by the elements of creation through the priestess. . After that, we had to take you to the four cardinal directions. We began with the North, where you were laid on the ground."

Da closes his eyes and concentrates.

"Spirits of the North, powers of winter, guardians of earth and stone, strength of wolf and badger, who you teach us of love and loyalty, great bear of the starry skies, Lady of the sacred womb, the rich soil of creation, bless this child with your gifts : true stability, security, nourishment, certainty, the source of rich and fertile creativity."

We then blessed you with a symbol of earth, a consecrated stone.

In the East, we held you up to the skies.

"Spirits of the East, powers of spring, of conception, regeneration, vision of falcon and blackbird's song, swallows' freedom flight, sylphs of the wind, breath of life, Lord of the rising sun and all new life, bless our child with your gifts : freedom, clarity, open hearted wisdom, pure inspiration, the power of listening. knowledge awakening, the magic of song. There, you were blessed with a symbol of air. We gave you a book about your namesake, *Aoife,* to read when you were older.

After that, in the South, I, your father held you in my arms.

"Spirits of the South, powers of summer, pride of stag, fire wit of fox, dragons of the land, sprites of the dancing flame, you who teach us of courage and the power of truth, Lord of the Greenwood, bless our child with your gifts : strength, vitality, clear vision, passion, the courage to be who she can truly be."

You were blessed with a symbol of fire, which for you was a lighted candle.

In the West, you were held by Mam.

"Spirits of the West, powers of autumn, wild cat and silent owl, stretching to hunt at dusk, wisdom of salmon and otter's play, undines of chuckling brook, devas - they're celestial beings - dance our love and emotion, Lady of the Seas, tides of being, bless this child with your gifts : flexibility, direction, love in perfect trust, flow of emotion, rich creativity."

You were blessed with symbol of water. We poured a liitle water on your forehead – which you weren't too keen on if I remember !!

Then, we returned to the circle and the priestess said another prayer. Mam and I had to explain why we gave you the name *Aoife.*

After that, witnessed by everyone there, the priestess asked us all to say your name and welcome you, using your name and saying it together.
Then we had celebratory food and drink. We had sandwiches, cake and champagne as a treat. The priestess blessed the feast and thanked everyone for attending the ceremony."

I ask Da about any conflicts between being a Druid parent and Mam being a Catholic parent, albeit that they are both True Believers.

Da thinks for a moment before answering me. "I'm sure you know that things do go wrong sometimes. Mam is probably more divided about being a True Believer and also a Catholic. She can't reveal much to Father O'Donnelly. He is open-minded about certain aspects where things tally. He christened you, which he might have refused to do. However, on other points, he can be very set in his ways. The Church has its rules, as you know and he has bent them a bit for our family and others. He knows we are good at heart. Although we might argue that being parents such as us can bring added pressure, there is a certain amount of light at the end of the tunnel. Druidry, or what the Church calls 'paganism' is growing in popularity as people search for answers."

"What kind of answers ?"

"Well, they might ask why does God allow, or accept, wars, or starvation, like in Africa and other third world countries ? The Church will argue it's because people are allowed free will. Although one of the ten commandments is 'thou shalt not kill', the Bible says that holy wars or wars to fight evil, like fighting the Nazis in World War Two, is acceptable, even necessary."

"At school we learned that Jesus said, "Truly I tell you, unless you change and become like little children, you will never enter the kingdom of heaven."

"I think children are born 'good'. 'Bad' or 'evil' is learned. That's why good parents should encourage love, kindness, concern for other people and so on."

"I think they have to have support and encouragement too. "

Da nods. "Encouraging children to have a positive attitude to life is very important. As parents we have to help shape your future, so we have to show them the way. You're lucky because you have your Otherworld sisters and friends as well."

"What about religion ?"

That is more complicated. We just have to be open and tolerant. I hope Mam and I have taught you to think for yourself and mull things over before you jump in with both feet."

We laugh together.

"We do have to be patient and tolerant of others' beliefs. We're in a minority. Mam and I do our best to look for ways to teach you values without compromising either of our belief systems. We had to look hard to find literature that we could share with you. Literature that also mirrors our religious paths. It could have been an awesome responsibility ! Luckily, you love books as much as me and you have always asked questions which we have tried, still do, our best to answer."

I feel a sense of pride. It's true I have always loved reading and writing, especially my journal.

"What I like," I tell Da, is that neither of you have ever tried to force anything down my throat. I've had the opportunity to consider options, even when I was quite little."

Now Da looks proud. "Thanks, sweetie."

We are quiet for several minutes, contemplating what's been said.

"One thing I think has been essential," continues Da, "is that a young person in your position should be presented with a number of possible all paths which lead to the Divine. There is no single pathway. All are valid. I hope you feel that we have allowed you access to other points of view. Otherwise, how else could you make an informed choice, now that you are older ?"

"I think you have, although I know I'm still on the journey, but learning all the time."

"That will continue for your whole life."

Back in my room I'm thinking of one thing that I particularly liked learning about . It was The Eightfold Wheel of the Year. I love the fact that it's based on the deep and mysterious connection between the Source of our individual Earthly lives and the source of the life of the planet, It's that connection which *Aoife* and the others have demonstrated to me."

Druidry recognises eight particular times during the yearly cycle which are significant and which are marked by eight special festivals.

I've learned much about these 8 times.

- 4 of them are solar and the other 4 are lunar. This is essential in creating a balanced system of interlocking male and female observances; procedures, ceremonies, or rites for a particular occasion. The cycle, the wheel, suggests a consistency. The solar observances are the ones that most people associate with modern-day Druidry. For example, particularly the Summer Solstice ceremonies at Stonehenge.

- At the Solstices, the Sun is revered at the point of its apparent 'death' at Midwinter and of its maximum power at the noon of the year when the days are longest. At the Equinoxes, day and night are balanced. At the Spring Equinox, the power of the sun is on the increase, and we celebrate the time of sowing seeds and of preparation for the gifts of Summer.

- At the Autumn Equinox, although day and night are of equal duration, the power of the sun is on the wane, and we give thanks for the gifts of the harvest and prepare for the darkness of Winter.

These 4 festivals are astronomical observances. Da has explained that we know they are ancient and that our ancestors marked them with ritual. The stone circles are oriented to their points of sunrise or sunset. When the circles were built, our ancestors had become a pastoral people, and times of sowing and reaping of crops were vitally important.

As well as the 4 astronomical, solar festivals, there are also 4 times in the year which have always been considered sacred. These were the times which were more associated with the livestock cycle, rather than the farming cycle. They are *Samhuinn, Imbolic, Beltane* and *Lughnasadh.*

The first was a time in late Autumn, 1st November, for slaughtering livestock when fodder was in short supply. The meat was then salted and stored. The second held on 1st February was when lambs began to be born. At *Beltane* on the 1st May it was the time of mating for livestock and of the passing of the livestock through the two *Beltane* fires for purification.

Here in Ireland, *Beltane* is the Celtic/Gaelic May Day festival. Most commonly it is held on 1st May, or sometimes halfway between the Spring equinox and Summer solstice. The last one, *Lughnasadh*, is on 1st August. It is the time which marked the link between the agricultural and the livestock cycle. That's when the harvest began and both human food and animal fodder were reaped and stored.

The two sets of festivals represent far more than just times which our ancestors chose to honour the plant and animal life-cycles . They are a representation of our thorough interconnectedness with both the animal and plant realms. That is central to the beliefs of the Otherworld and something that we humans have to learn, especially in our modern world where living in towns and cities and working in industry and commerce, take us away from our natural roots.

Both *Aoife* and *Banba* have emphasised to me that these festivals show how interwoven the life of our mind and our body with the planet really is and should be. Earth, Sun and Moon. It's what we True Believers aim for - the integration of such festival times to mark a potent conjunction of Time and Place, both here, in the Otherworld, in the Multiverse.

The veil between these worlds and the world of our ancestors is drawn aside on these nights. Things become clearer. Those who are preparing to die and be reborn know that at these times, their journeys can be made in safety .

The Druid rites, mirror those of The Otherworld. They are concerned with making contact with the spirits of the departed. Those who are reborn have lived on Earth and experienced life. They become teachers and are consulted as sources of guidance and inspiration. It's why True Believers (not all of whom are Druids) do not fear death.

The dark moon, that's the time when you can't see the moon in the sky, is the phase of the moon which rules this time. It represents a time in which what we see with our eyes in the physical world, needs to be covered over, so that we can see into the Otherworld.

In this way our dead are honoured and celebrated, not as the dead, but as the living spirits of loved ones and of guardians who hold the root-wisdom of the people.

Da has also explained how, with the coming of Christianity, this festival on October 31st was turned into 'All Hallows' – what we call today Halloween. All Saints Day is on November 1st and All Souls on November 2nd. Da says if you look at the history of such festivals, it becomes clear how Christianity itself built on ancient Celtic or pagan foundations.

- The 21st of December is the Winter Solstice The Druids call it *Alban Arthan* , which means the Light of Arthur. This is the time of death and rebirth. The sun moves away and makes way for the longest night. Our own spiritual journey has completed its annual cycle and the light is discarded. In the darkness we have the opportunity to discard things which have been holding us back in some way. One lamp is lit by using a flint and it's raised up on the Druid's crook facing East. In this way, the year is reborn and a new cycle begins.

Although the Bible says that Jesus was born in the Spring, the early Church chose to move the official time to celebrate his birthday to the time of the Midwinter Solstice. Da said it's one example of how Christianity built on the foundations of ancient beliefs.

- The next Festival, called *Imbolc* is on February 2nd, or the evening of February 1st. Every 6 weeks or so, Druids have the opportunity to step out of our normal daily lives, so that we can honour the conjunction of Place and Time. *Imbolc* represents the first of 3 Spring celebrations. This is the time when snowdrops first appear. The snow melts and lambs begin to be born. The Winter is behind us. In the Druid tradition it's a gentle, beautiful festival in which the Mother Goddess is honoured with eight candles rising out of the water at the centre of the ceremonial circle. For children, *Imbolc* marks the time of early childhood, up to about 7 years old. Seeds are planted at this time.

- The Goddess that rules *Samhuinn* is the *Cailleach*. She has several names, the Grey Hag, the Mountain Mother and the Dark Woman of Knowledge. But by the time *Imbolc* comes round, the Goddess has become *Brigid*, the Goddess of poets, healers and midwives.It's a time for poetry and song and praising the Goddess in her many forms. The Christian Church developed this festival and called it Candlemas. I know from Religious Studies at school, that this is the time of the Presentation of Christ in the Temple. It's a time to go to Church where priests bless the candles.

- May is the time for the Spring Equinox. That's the times of equal day and night, The forces of the Light are increasing.

At the centre of the trio of Spring *Festas*, *Alban Eilir,* the Light of the Earth, marks the signs of Spring in nature and the time to sow seeds. For children, like me, it marks our late childhood, up to about 14 years old. I am, like my friends and classmates, in the Spring of our lives. This is a time where we increase our abilities and powers so that we can begin to organise our lives with skill and accomplishment.

- May 1st is also *Beltane*. It marks the time of our adolescence and early womanhood, as in my case. Manhood for boys. Spring is in full bloom. At one time, twin fires used to be lit for the cattle to pass through after their long winter confinement. If cattle jumped over the fires it would be good for people hoping for a child or good fortune. Today, dancing round the maypole is traditional on May Day, although this is a custom which seems to be dying out. It's to celebrate the fertility of the land and it's a bit like the ritual circle dances that took place in stone circles.

- June 21st is the Summer Solstice, *Alban Hefin*, The Light of the Shore, by June 21st or 22nd. The dates for each of the solar festivals vary each year because the events are astronomical, not man-made, like the Roman calendar. Light is at its maximum, and this is the time of the longest day. It is at this time that the Druids hold the most complex ceremony. It starts at midnight on the eve of the Solstice when a vigil is held through the night with everyone sitting around the Solstice fire. As daylight breaks, the Dawn Ceremony marks the time of the sun's rising on this his most powerful day. At noon a further ceremony is held.

- August 1st is *Lughnasadh*. Six weeks later is the time of *Lughnasadh* on August 1st, marking the beginning of harvest time. The hay has been gathered in and the time for reaping wheat and barley is due to begin. It's a time of gathering together with fun and games, as well as marriages. Marriages contracted at this time can be annulled at the same time the following year, giving the couple a 'trial period'. Da always takes the mickey out of Mam, because they didn't do this. Not that's they'd have changed their minds I think because they are very happy together. In some areas a flaming wheel is sent rolling down the hillside at this time to symbolise the dropping of the year towards Winter. In the Druid ceremony a wheel is passed around the circle in symbol of the turning year. The Christian version of this festival is called Lammas. The word Lammas comes from *hlafmasse* which means 'loaf-mass' . It's because bread is offered that has been made from newly harvested grain. I know, of course, from both Mam and school, that Mass is a reference to the Mass where Holy Communion is given as a piece of bread soaked in wine. It symbolises the Body and Blood of Christ.

- September 21st is the Autumn Equinox. It's called *Alban Elfed* or 'Light of the Water'. in the Druid tradition. It represents the second of the harvest festivals – this time marking the end of harvest-time, just as Lughnasadh marked its beginning. Again day and night are equally balanced as they were at the time of the

Spring Equinox, but soon the nights will grow longer than the days and Winter will be with us. In the ceremony we give thanks for the fruits of the earth and for the goodness of the Mother Goddess.

That's how the circle / the wheel completes itself as we come back to the time of *Samhuinn*, the time of death and of rebirth.

I had a conversation with Da and asked him, "What does it mean to celebrate these festivals? Do we just want to revive the old customs so they're not forgotten ?"

"We do want to keep the festival celebrations alive, that's true. They are traditional and we respect that. It's not the only reason though. It's more deep-seated than that. For instance, Christmas and New Year are vital to our psychic health because they give us some measure of the passage of our lives. It's much the same for Christians."

"But Christians are celebrating the birth of Jesus."

"True, but that's a good thing. We can all celebrate these special times. The idea is to develop our sense of spirituality. We look for an increasing sense of peace and knowing our place in this world, as well as the Otherworld. Christians would relate that to being on Earth and living your life in a good way in order to get a place in Heaven."

I'm beginning to understand the basis of our beliefs better. It's becoming more clear. It's reassuring for me that both Da's and Mam's beliefs may be different in some ways, like Druid and Christian, but at a spiritual level, it's about being good and kind. Mam has said having Otherworldly sisters helps us to find the light within our hearts and how to make our links with the natural world.

I remember *Banba* told me a lovely story about how she sometimes adopts human form, goes to market where animals are being bought for slaughter . She takes them away, then giving them their freedom in an Otherworldly dimension. Mam and Da are vegetarians, as am I, so I love this story.

There are many tales like this which I learned when I was younger. Another one is about a dragon and a unicorn. A king is destroying the forest where his family and all his subjects live. The two creatures make themselves known to the princess, his daughter. They take her to listen to the trees, plants and creatures of the forest. They tell her that the forest is as much home to her and her family as it is to them. If the forest is destroyed, her father will have killed the very environment they live in and rely on. The princess returns to the palace and explains this to her father. He sees the sense in what she says and stops the destruction.

I remember also that Mam and Da told me that when I was born , they couldn't stop looking at me. They said I had a wise look in my eyes. They both realised that they were overwhelmed by the realisation that they were totally responsible for the safety and education of another human being. It was going to be their responsibility to teach me how to be a good and kind member of the Worlds that True Believers cherish. They knew that they should provide a strong foundation for my journey through life.

They have both shown me that no one path is forced down anyone's throat. All children's paths that lead to the Divine are valid. I think they have allowed me to access other points of view. I see this in my convent school. Sometimes things interlink. Other times it's hard to make them fit together. It's like a jigsaw puzzle, finding where the pieces go.

Da says the more I am presented with, the easier it will be make informed choices. They always guide and support, but, I know as I get older, I will be making more and more decisions myself.

I know from Da that the Isle of Man is famous for being the capital of the Druids since way back. It's one of the 6 (multiple of 3) Celtic nations, and has been under Norse, Scottish and English control. Despite that, it has been self-governing for much of the past thousand years. During the Iron Age, Celtic influence began to accumulate on the island. According to local folklore, the first man in the Isle of Man had 3 legs !

I know that being a Druid means a journey of spiritual development. The use of ancient forms of medicine to promote healing and rejuvenation are also important.

I have learnt from Da that in medieval times, Irish writers wrote about the Druids, but this was written hundreds of years after the ancient Druids had disappeared, so the accuracy of the information is questionable. Apparently, there is nothing to refer to which was actually written by a Druid or by people from the same society. How mysterious ! Could records have been destroyed when Christianity came along ?

I read that the Greeks and Romans thought of the Druids as priests and scientists, but Druid craft to the Irish is more about magic and spells. Since the Isle of Man is in what's called the 'Irish cultural province' that is also the way the Manx people would have seen Druids. Nowadays things are more complex.

A modern Druid ceremony

Religious and magical powers mattered a lot in ancient times, especially in Ireland, so the Druids would have been a powerful sector of society.

In the 16th century, the book tells me, the Scots loved the Druids because they were at the time best friends with the French who favoured the Druids. The Welsh and the English ignored them because they didn't want to be associated with the people in Scotland.

By the 18th century, everybody loved them ! In the 19th century it changed again. The Scots started to ignore Druids, whereas the Welsh started to love them and the English started to hate them ! Da laughed and said that is a fascinating overview of national identity and how it's changed over time !

The Isle of Man lies between all these countries, so the Manx people used to favour the English simply because England was its biggest trading partner. It would have seemed the most sensible thing to do at the time in terms of money and exchange of goods.

In modern times, Druids focus on some of the more benevolent views of ancient Druidry. People are usually attracted to it of they are those who want to change things by bringing more spirituality into their lives. I love that idea. It has become more and more important to me since I first came in touch with the *Aoife, Banba, Epona* and *Faoladh*, my wolf protector.

Da and I were discussing Stonehenge not so long ago. Again, we don't really know if people ever worshipped there, although it is perfectly possible that they did.

Stonehenge

There is also another kind of modern Druidry which is more radical. Druids now take action against things they see as damaging to the environment. For example, protesting against new roads and building work which cut swathes across countryside, or dig up an area of natural beauty, endangering plants and animals alike. Da has explained that, in a similar way, ancient Druids would have opposed the arrival of Roman towns and roads.

The author of the book suggests, "We have no idea if an ancient Druid would approve of this modern interpretation of Druidry, but I would like to think so."

Me too !

Date: 2021

Aoife came to me recently. I'm pleased that she approves the journal extracts which I have chosen for my book. *Aoife* is as lovely as ever. Of course, she doesn't age in the way we humans do because she is able to choose any form. I have always noticed that *Aoife* is one who knows how to dress for each season. Today she is in green, blended with all the colours of summer flowers. She sparkles and as the light catches her gown and she moves around, the colours become iridescent . I have always known that she carries magic in her core.

Of course, she can also be invisible when she desires. Her abilities to blend in to any society, because she is from the realm of The Otherworld, means she can be born into any species, any version of reality at any place in the time-continuum. Over my lifetime I have experienced many examples of this in her.

She has helped me to fix things that have gone wrong where she can. I have always treated her with the greatest of respect as a protector. We children of Adam and Eve, as Catholics might call us, have free will. This should not mean anarchy. Sadly, in this world today I see much argument and threat of violence everywhere. It is my firm belief that we need to reconnect with nature. We must respect others, be they people, creatures or any natural phenomena. Maybe humanity must show a little more humility. We are a dot in the Multiverse.

Those from The Otherworld have a way of looking right into our souls, as if they are a book open for the reading. They ease their way into your being with more than ordinary words. Their communication has a greater effect than any drug.
I discovered that the changes in their appearance were dependent on what I needed to see so as to be at ease. They could look like any race or gender, any size. So asking me what they really look like is futile. Mam says even they themselves may not know all the possibilities. They are not afraid. It's second nature for them.

I have learnt that their lore is our law. My Otherworldly companions and, equally, my parents have shown me that reading and storytelling are an essential part of building a good mind and spirit. I have learnt that humans must take care of each other and our planet. For in this lore of all worlds, in this nexus, magic happens; shared and pure. Perhaps you might even call them miracles. However we define it, these gifts come to those who will do good with them. Learn and absorb the lore and you will have both order and freedom.

Through my experiences, I hope that one day soon, humans will choose to be humankind. It 's Alexandre Dumas, French writer (1802 – 1870) whose motto for his famous Three Musketeers, "All for one and one for all, united we stand divided we fall." expresses what I mean in a nutshell.

Modern 20th century humans walk the ground they pollute and ask it to sustain them with its bounty. As they become adults, they grow deaf and blind in the heart and mind to nature's needs. Nature gave us life, yet we abuse it more than ever. The doorway to our wonderful, natural world should be a mirror for the energy of our integrity of spirit. If you come to adulthood with an openness of mind and spirit, you will see the magical realm of nature and its beauty. Respecting and caring for our planet is how we make it safe and fit for future generations. Rid ourselves of our toxins until they are no more and let the warmth of the sunshine into our souls.

I have whisked myself and my readers through a lifetime of happenings and beliefs. For me, the journey back through my journal has been a voyage of exploration and a reminder of, sometimes a re-awakening to, things forgotten or half-remembered over a half-century.

There is more. Once the child *Aoife* has grown into a young woman, a whole 'other' life is revealed. I think for now though, this is a time to stop and reflect.

In this first part of Aoife's journal she has looked at extracts from 1965 until 1969 – from her 12th birthday until she is 16 years old.

After her 16th birthday, things begin to change and develop in Aoife's life and her contact with The Otherworld.

The second part of Aoife's journal will be published later this year.

Printed in Great Britain
by Amazon